Steep Cliffs

Steep Cliffs

Alex Pattillo

Writers Club Press
San Jose New York Lincoln Shanghai

Steep Cliffs

Writers Club Press
an imprint of iUniverse.com, Inc.

For information address:
iUniverse.com, Inc.
5220 S 16th, Ste. 200
Lincoln, NE 68512
www.iuniverse.com

ISBN: 0-595-15716-5

Printed in the United States of America

Introduction

In 1837, a small town called Terminus was founded in the Georgia territories. The town rapidly grew into a busy trade and transportation center. In 1845, a railroad engineer named J. Edgar Thomas renamed the town Atlanta, and it served as a Confederate supply depot. The union troops led by General William T. Sherman captured Atlanta in 1864 and burned most of its buildings. However, the city never lost its industrial expansion and construction growth. Today, Atlanta is one of the fastest-growing cities in the nation.

In the 1960's, Atlanta's Martin Luther King Junior led blacks in the Civil Rights movement. In 1996, Atlanta hosted the Centennial Olympic Games. Some say Atlanta is always under construction. The traffic seems infinite, as the city's population continues to increase more rapidly than ever.

Through the years, religion had also grown in Atlanta. But, the 1990's became the decade of unparalleled church growth. Churches all over the city started renovating, remodeling, and adding increased space. Large youth groups became more popular than ever. Therefore, in all aspects, Atlanta is continually under construction.

Chapter 1

The gym was alive. The colored spotlights whirled across the audience who were screaming, clapping, dancing, crying, and singing along with the young band playing "futuristic church music" on the platform. The band consisted of all high school students—a guy playing the piano, two with electric guitars, one with an acoustic guitar, a guy on drums, and three girls singing into microphones; the guys on guitars were singing also. Drums and guitars, male and female, everyone in the band shared something special. They were all in bellbottoms, the female vocalists all had long straight blond hair, and the guys were wearing bellbottoms as well along with shaggy hair covering their ears. The bands' outward appearance wasn't the thing that made it special; they all somehow shared a yearning, burning passion for what they were doing up on the platform. And, although the music was being played and sung by unprofessional teenagers, the audience didn't seem to really care.

The crowd, all high school students, was moved by the music, there was no mistaking that. The unique thing about their mutual enjoyment of this gathering was that they seemed to have nothing else in common. The crowd consisted of a mixture of all different types of teenagers. Some were preppy and some were the "dorks" of the school. Some were popular buff football players with varsity athlete jackets on, and others were hippies wasted on every illegal drug available. Some, especially the football players, seemed a little uncomfortable with the whole atmosphere. While there were a few elderly teachers with tight lips and arms crossed observing everything that went on "to make sure everything stays in order," and other teachers who walked out of the gym complaining that the music was too loud. There was certainly something being planted at that moment in everyone attending this strange gathering.

The music itself was amazing. It sounded like regular, secular radio music, but the words were church words. It was weird to everyone. The students called it "rock 'n' roll hymns" or "Christian Beatles." It was definitely Christian music that they had written themselves. The students loved the beat, but most of the faculty hated it. There was not really a name to describe the event, so the students came up with the word "Gathering."

The music ended with a long, vibrating electric sound and the applause started—a long screaming applause. But the crowd didn't seem to be applauding the song, but something else, something the faculty couldn't quite figure out.

As the band wound down and began leaving the platform heading down the wooden steps, a recognizable figure with a quick, heavy stride stomped up the steps and appeared on the platform. John Benson was a high school student. The crowd immediately started roaring and clapping with joy as the teenager stepped onto the platform. Looking at the subgroups of people in the audience—the football players, the dorks, and the hippies—John didn't seem to fit into any one stereotype. Instead, he was his own person, and everyone wanted to be in his group. He was way too sociable and confident to be a dork, he was too little and skinny to be a popular football player, and he was too down-to-earth to be a hippie. He was dressed in leather sandals, plaid bellbottoms, and a loose white tee shirt. His appearance made him popular with the girls. He had an average face with calm green eyes that had the appeal of a trusting puppy. His wavy, dark brown hair hung over his eyebrows, over his ears, and curled at his collar in a shaggy fashion.

John continued his long, casual, trademark stride across the platform until he reached the microphone. The crowd quieted down. He quickly surveyed their faces. In the front row sat John's grandmother and his mom. And a few seats over sat his very special friend, "friend-girl" he called her, because he wasn't interested in romance at this point. He smiled; pleased to see her there.

In a crisp voice he spoke, "I don't know what made you all come tonight, but praise the Lord you're here."

The crowd cheered in response.

John continued, "As we approach the year 1965 in," he glanced at his watch, "in two hours, we want to really praise God with every cell, every atom, every ounce of muscle in our body and lift Him up as we thank Him for this wonderful year."

More cheering.

"In the process of doing that, let me refresh your memory as to how this gathering got started. Last year in my sophomore year, I had this vision in my head of starting something different and new and something that would glorify God. Something different from the same old, boring church services every single Sunday-something deeper, more spiritual. Soon, I started talking with other Christians at this school about it. I told them all I wanted to do, and then came the question of money. It was going to be expensive to pay for all the lighting and instruments. Then came the question of popularity. You know, how would this affect our. popularity. Would people love this? Will people hate this? And what about the law? You know, three years ago, that new law passed that we can't pray in school.

"So we started with a small Bible study with only eight people in the library after school on Tuesdays. And look at what God has done in only one year. He grew our small Bible study with eight people to a big gathering with 1,076 people in one year! Folks, we have counted 1,076 people tonight. And that's the most we've ever gotten."

Now everyone cheered.

"But don't forget, this is not a festival, this is not a performance, this is not a show, this is worship—simple pure worship. Yes, we have grown and we do have more equipment now, but there is one thing that has never and *will* never change. And that's the heart of worship. If the heart of worship *ever* fails in you, then don't come. Don't come. If you are coming here just to hang out with your friends and goof off and just for the heck of it, then don't come."

The crowd grew a little uncomfortable but still knew he was right.

John smiled to loosen up the audience and started his preaching. He preached about half an hour about the heart of worship. Then he closed with a quick word of prayer, and the band came up again to play a few more songs, closing by midnight.

The lights brightened over the crowd, and they began to stand up as they talked and moved toward the exit. John immediately made his way toward his grandmother. He smiled and asked nicely, "So what did you think?"

She stared at him with her frozen gaze until she said, "If you expect to succeed in anything, you have to please the crowd." She started to turn away.

John stepped out in front of her, "What do you mean?"

She raised her voice a little, "What I mean is all that talk of the heart of worship or whatever you said. Now you listen here, if you want to make people follow you and your little gathering, then you must at least be engaging. And that music! Never in my life have I heard worse music than that. God doesn't like to listen to rock 'n' roll!"

John still remained calm but raised his voice a little to make a point, "I'm just saying and doing what is right."

"You're just doing the opposite, that's what you're doing." She turned to John's mother who he didn't even notice was standing there, "Take me home."

John's mom escorted her toward the exit and looked at him with a sad expression that he hoped meant, "I'm sorry." Then, he felt a hand land gently on his shoulder, turned around and saw Mary.

She smiled, "I think you did great."

John always loved her voice. It was so soft and so delicate with a slight Southern accent. He smiled to the side and exhaled, "Thanks. You're the only one who encourages me with this thing. I'm just doing what's right."

"Well, I think you're doing just the right thing."

He smiled even more now, "Thanks."

"Well, I must be getting home now. I'll call you." Then she turned and left. John felt a chill go up his spine. *Was the heart of worship topic really that bad?* He looked up at the gym ceiling. *God, show me what to do.*

Chapter 2

Thirty-four years later.

The moving truck finished unloading the last bit of furniture into a small, one-story cottage. A middle-aged woman signed the bill and handed it to the moving truck driver. With a courteous smile, he said, "Have a nice day Mrs. Benson."

Though exhausted, she smiled back, "You too."

Then he drove off.

Mary Benson turned around and looked at the little cottage. She had to admit to herself, it was quaint. She would soon plant some pretty flowers and make a garden in the front lawn. But she had to finish moving in first. She opened the white, wooden, creaky door that slammed with the pull of the spring attached to it. She found her husband at the breakfast table with his head buried in his arms.

She walked towards him speaking with her slight Southern accent, "John, do you want to get something to eat somewhere?"

John lifted up his head slowly; his eyes were red from exhaustion. A nice looking man with salt-and-pepper gray hair, a calm face, and a collared shirt hanging over some blue jeans, he answered in a tired voice, "Sure. Where are the kids?"

"In their rooms."

John stood up and stretched. Then he walked down the hallway and entered an empty room. There stood a beautiful, slender, brown-haired sixteen-year-old girl and a skinny brown-haired ten-year-old boy.

"Amber, Will, we're going to go eat somewhere."

Amber spoke up, "Dad, there's nothing good to eat in Atlanta."

"I'm sure we'll find something in this big city."

Amber let out a frustrating grunt, "What was wrong with living in our nice, small town in Tennessee anyway?"

"Honey, we've been through this over and over again. I'd rather be living in Tennessee, but God is calling me to become the new pastor of this huge church here in Atlanta."

Amber exhaled slowly. She could not really argue with that. But, at the same time, she wanted him to know how she felt. She grew up in a home, *her* home in Tennessee all her life. Now she had to watch some strangers buy and move into her home, and her family was living in a new city leaving all their friends behind.

Overwhelmed, she walked out of the room and went somewhere to be all by herself.

Will looked up at his father, "Dad, why is Amber always like that? She used to be so nice."

John shook his head, "She's just going through a lot right now. Moving is not a cool thing for teenage girls."

* * *

The next week passed with no improvements in family relations. Everything was still in boxes and everyone was still grumpy. It was about mid-afternoon, the summer day was actually a bit cooler today, the birds chirped happily, and the window garden by the breakfast table was already looking beautiful. John was sipping earl gray tea and eating scones and crème that Mary had made herself. She noticed that John was unusually quiet. She knew what he was thinking about. She sat down in the chair next to him and faced him, "So are you ready?"

He just stared at his tea, "I haven't done this sort of thing in years."

She put her arm around him, "You'll do great. I know you will. I know for a fact that you have a gift from God in leading people. You showed it in high school."

"But this is totally different. This is a five thousand member church with lots of money and big expectations, and I'm going to be the pastor."

"There's no difference. You even said so yourself back in high school. Obeying God is obeying God wherever you are."

Once again, Mary succeeded in encouraging him. His calm innocent eyes sparkled and a smile crept onto his face, "Thanks. Let's just pray right now."

* * *

The Bensons' aged, gray Volvo sedan drove across the expressway. John was driving and Mary sat in the passenger seat staring out the window, obviously thinking about something. Will sat in the back marveling at the cars that flew by. Amber sat tolerantly in the back as well. Everyone was dressed up. John was wearing a coat and tie. The sun was setting behind the trees. Everything was silent. Not a word was being uttered during the whole long ride.

Finally, Amber broke the silence, "Dad?"

John answered, "Yes?"

"Um, I've heard that this is a very liberal church. Is that right?"

"Yes, that's right. But we're going to go full throttle with the Word of God into this church."

That was the last thing that was said. The Volvo turned off an exit and started down a road. John followed the signs that were marked, *"People of God."*

After making some more turns, the church finally came into view. John knew it was big, but not *this* big. The church appeared to be the size of a big mall. It was primarily made of stucco, stone, and marble, but you could see where they had added on. It didn't even look like a church. The front was just a huge stucco block like an Imax Theater with a faint cross engraved in the middle. The grounds were beautifully landscaped, and there was a beautiful fountain with water spraying in high rainbow patterns in the front. An expensive marble sign with *"People of God"* emblazoned boldly across it stood close to the road as they turned into the driveway. The church even had its own logo engraved prominently on the sign.

John pulled into the parking lot where men in reflecting orange coats directed him into parking garage number six. Hundreds of cars were already parked. And these weren't just ordinary cars. Most were very expensive cars. Will counted three Rolls-Royces before they found an open space. They parked, got out, and started making their way to the sanctuary. The back of the church was all glass like an art museum. There were two sets of double doors—one for going in and one for going out. The Benson family got in line with all the other people going in.

Slowly, they made their way inside. It was very crowded, but no one talked. It was as if no one knew each other. John noticed a gift shop over to the right with crowds of people *shopping*—shopping inside a church! John felt more uncomfortable than ever. Was this a church of God or a church of man?

"John."

John turned around and saw Reverend Johnson, the current pastor of the church. He wasn't much older than John, but already had gray hair. He and John had known each other since high school. He held out his hand, "Good to see you."

John shook his hand, "Good to see you too."

"Your family can go ahead and sit in the reserved seats up front. Please follow me."

John gave Mary an assuring nod and followed Reverend Johnson.

Reverend Johnson spoke up, "Isn't it amazing? God is really working here at the People of God."

John nodded, "Yep, it looks that way."

"Well, as you know, I'm moving on to start another People of God out west and I need a very forward-thinking man to take my place as pastor of this church. I've prayed that God will show me the right man and I believe that man is you. What you did with the Gathering in high school still amazes me."

John smiled politely, "Oh thank you."

They came to a back door into the sanctuary. Reverend Johnson opened it and led John on platform. He spontaneously caught his breath when he entered. The platform floor was stained wood and was huge. It seemed that every musical instrument ever made was sitting on it. The backdrop was a manufactured indoor jungle with an artificial sun and clouds made by fog machines. Behind the branches was a big white cross. John looked at the congregation. Red theater seats with drink holders in the armrests lined the floor space. There were three balconies making it possible for the auditorium to accommodate several thousand people. It was already packed with people wearing their casual summer clothes and more kept on coming in with drinks and popcorn that they were buying in the back. He could see the rest of the Benson family sitting right in the front row.

Reverend Johnson led John to a chair on the platform. He sat down in it feeling horribly oppressed by the atmosphere. The church band started warming up. John saw a huge screen drop down behind him with the words to the songs and media slides flashing at the crowd. The band started playing. Everyone in the congregation stood up. The band played good music that John liked, and it sounded very professional, almost too professional. He looked out at the congregation. Yes, they were standing all right, but none of them, not one, was singing or even clapping. They were supposed to be singing, but they just stared like zombies, as if they were accustomed to the spectacle and perhaps even bored. Even the band sounded methodical and bored. Actually, dead was an accurate word to describe how the band sounded. No one seemed to be enjoying the music. In fact, while the music was supposed to evoke feeling, the atmosphere was devoid of feeling. The song was short, followed by a few more songs that sounded redundant. Throughout all of them, the audience and the singers lacked life. Although they sounded professional, they also sounded depressed.

Finally, the music was over and the congregation sat down. Reverend Johnson stood and went to the podium. He spoke in a pastor-like voice amplified by the professional sound boxes and perfect acoustics. "Today I have the special privilege of introducing our new pastor. But before we get into that, let me make a few announcements." He put on his reading glasses and unfolded a piece of paper, "Uh, all books sold at the gift shop have a fifteen percent discount all this week. We are currently out of t-shirts, because the company we have been using has declared bankruptcy. We apologize for the inconvenience for those of you who had placed orders. We're looking for another distributor now. Uh, this is addressed to the children especially—please do not throw pennies into the main water fountain. The pennies are getting stuck in the drain and clogging it up. And one more thing, the genuine wooden railings going down the aisles are very attractive. However, we ask that you do not touch them because the fingerprints smudge the beautiful shine.

"Now let me introduce to you our new pastor." There was actually a drum roll as Reverend Johnson spoke,

"John Benson was born and raised in a small town in Tennessee. When he attended public high school, God gave him a vision to establish a weekly gathering. It grew from an eight person Bible study to a 1,076 people gathering of praise and worship in only one year. After Seminary, he returned to his hometown to pastor a small church. He married his high school sweetheart, Mary, and they have two children, Amber and Will. Most importantly, I have known him since those high school days and know that he will lead this church in the right direction. So please, welcome John Benson."

There was a soft civilized applause as John stood up and walked to the podium. He started speaking in his usual crisp voice, "Good evening. I am delighted to be here…" Then he gave a simple sermon about God's grace. It only lasted for about fifteen minutes, and then he ended with a short prayer and sat back down. The band immediately set back up their equipment. The same process happened again as the dead audience stood and stared again.

John just sat there humiliated with his sermon. *Why can't I preach?* Once the music was over, everyone rose immediately from their chairs, lined up, and walked out. John did not know how so many people got out so fast. They must have been eager to go buy some discounted books and be first in line at lunch.

John shook hands with Reverend Johnson, motioned to his family, and walked speedily out of the building. No one they passed by even looked at him, much less offered thanks for the message. He felt like an outsider, a total stranger. The Bensons got into their car and made their way out of the parking deck and into the slowly moving line-up of cars.

When they finally made it onto the expressway, Mary spoke, "So how did you feel about your sermon?"

The answer was quick and simple, "They're dead."

Amber spoke up, "You know, Dad, you don't have to take this job."

"Sweetie, I have to take responsibility for doing what I believe God has said to do."

Again, the car was silent. It was so strange because the family always talked in the car. But today, they didn't. When John was upset, everyone was upset. That's how it worked. So, they drove off without another word uttered.

Chapter 3

It was late August now, and Atlanta was hotter than ever. The public school bell rang throughout the building. All the doors in the hallway flung open as Hispanics, blacks, whites and kids of mixed race rushed out and headed to the cafeteria. It was a fairly nice school. It was big and overly populated though. It had not changed in thirty years. The floor was made of hard brown tiles, the air conditioning was an afterthought, the cheap walls were chipping, and the lockers were old and rusty. Apparently, the janitors did not bother to dust the place or get rid of the cobwebs in the corners or try to get rid of that rust mixed with mildew smell.

After the elementary students rushed out the door leading to the cafeteria, all was quiet except for the echoing footsteps of Will Benson making his way by himself to the cafeteria. It was his first day in a new school so he had an excuse not to be hanging out with anybody, but he had always carried the reputation of "the quiet kid with no friends." He was always quiet, never popular in his old school. His best friend was his dad.

Will approached the double cafeteria doors. The line for the food was already overflowing outside the doors, as he took his place in the back. Oh no. Standing in line right in front of him was "the gang" Will had noticed when he first walked into the classroom. He knew from his first glimpse of them that they were up to no good. The leader guy, Jimmy, turned around and looked at Will. Jimmy was bigger than everyone else in fifth grade. He was tall, somewhat chubby, strong, and seemed to tower over Will making Will feel like he was some sort of mouse. And on top of all that, Jimmy was eleven-years-old and was supposed to be in sixth grade. His hair was shaved which added the bad boy look to his large stature. His two followers turned around and stood next to Jimmy as he faced Will. They were a bit smaller than Jimmy, but still taller and bigger than Will. Everyone was taller and bigger than Will. He inherited his dad's shortness and skinniness, and that did not help his popularity.

Jimmy spoke, "Look. It's the new kid." His followers nodded in response.

Still looking at Will, Jimmy asked his followers, "Should we give him the new kid treatment?"

One of his followers answered, "I think we should."

Jimmy mocked very effectively, "I think we should."

Will swallowed and cleared his throat, "What's the new kid treatment?"

A mischievous smile formed on Jimmy's fat sweaty face, "Trust me, you'll like it."

Before Will could do anything, Jimmy put his arm around his shoulder acting friendly as he escorted him across the gym floor. His followers followed him smirking and chuckling the whole time while Jimmy spoke friendly remarks to Will. They went across the gym and into the boy's locker room. Will's heart pounded harder. He knew "treatments" in the locker rooms were not good.

Suddenly all at once, Jimmy's friendliness vanished and before Will knew it, Jimmy's followers grabbed his legs, as Jimmy knocked him down on the tiled floor and pinned him. Will squirmed, but the harder he squirmed, the tighter the pain was around his neck. Jimmy's gang snatched him up from the floor and held him in the air with his legs up and his head dangling.

Instinctively, Will knew exactly what was going to happen. He squirmed and cried, "No, no! Please!"

But Jimmy's gang wasn't listening. They walked over to one of the toilets. Will was facing the ugly toilet water. He was so close that he could smell the aroma.

Jimmy's was counting rhythmically in the background, "1-2-3!"

Will held his breath and closed his eyes as his head splashed into the water. He was kicking, struggling, trying desperately to fight his way free, but it was no use. Now, he could hear nothing except for the deep silence of being under liquid. His legs grew weak, and he lost his strength to struggle any longer. He continued holding his breath while the world seemed to fade away. He was about to lose consciousness, as he started seeing nothing but white light. And, suddenly, his head was lifted out of the toilet water, and the nightmare became reality again. He opened his eyes and opened his mouth gasping for air. Water dripped from his face into his mouth. The taste was nauseating. Before he could get enough air, his head was again forced down into the toilet water.

This time he was not prepared. Dirty water poured into his mouth, and he swallowed. He was choking on it and yet, he couldn't breathe anyway. His head was again yanked out, but this time Will was thrown onto the tiled floor. He started gagging and coughing uncontrollably. Water squirted out of his mouth and nose, as he began heaving and vomiting all over the floor. Jimmy's gang was celebrating the accomplishment of their goal as they laughed and taunted.

Jimmy strutted out the door and his gang quickly followed. They didn't want to miss lunch, as they left Will on the floor trying hard not to but unable to avoid painful sobs.

* * *

Amber's high school was a little nicer than Will's elementary school. It still had the same worn, cheerless atmosphere and multi-racial student body, but it was cleaner and had a nicer campus with trees and sitting areas.

It was her lunchtime too, but she had an easier time fitting in than her brother. She walked smoothly and gracefully across the cafeteria wearing tight blue jeans and a white sleeveless shirt that hung from her shoulders on spaghetti straps. Her brown shiny hair hung loosely on her back a little below her shoulders. She was wearing a lot of makeup, maybe too much. But Amber's goal was to attract the guys, and she was doing a good job. She knew all the guys were checking her out, and she didn't mind it at all. She decided to skip lunch, as she sat down next to the "popular girls" and started getting to know them. They were all dressed like she was and all enjoyed attracting the guys too.

Amber smiled, "Hey, I'm Amber."

A girl sitting next to her with blond hair and blue eyes turned around and faced Amber. She smiled too, "Hey. I'm Meagan." She pointed to the three other girls with her, "And that's Jessica, Kate, and Julia."

They waved at Amber who waved back. Then, something caught her eye. Sitting at the table next to them was a handsome guy with a strong jaw, short black hair, and built, wearing an undershirt to show his muscles off. He looked popular by the way he was talking with other built guys.

Meagan leaned into Amber's ear, "What are you looking at?"

Amber kept her eyes on him, "That cute guy over there."

Meagan looked her way, "Oh that's Jason. He's such a hunk."

"Does he have a girlfriend?"

"Not currently, no."

Amber kept staring at him. Jason looked back at her and they made eye contact for a brief second until Amber turned away embarrassed, "He saw me."

Meagan replied, "Aw, that's alright. He's used to having girls stare at him all the time."

After school was over, everyone did their own thing. Some went to sports activities, others sat around and talked, and some went home.

Amber, on the other hand, had something else in mind. She was on a search for Jason. She paced around the school keeping her eyes peeled until she saw Meagan and her three friends. Amber walked quickly towards them, "Do you have any idea where Jason would be right now?"

They all looked at each other and shrugged. Kate spoke up, "Probably in the weight room." The others nodded.

Meagan whispered into Amber's ear, "You should talk to him. I'm sure he'll like you."

Amber smiled. It was no big deal. She was used to talking to guys like this. She waved a quick goodbye and headed towards the weight room. As she was passing through the gym, she spotted Jason walking out of the weight room in gym shorts and a tee shirt. There was no one else in the gym except for Jason and Amber, as they continued walking towards each other. Now was a good time for her to talk to him.

They got closer and closer to each other until they were within talking distance. Amber smiled, put on her model walk, and spoke first, "Hey."

Jason replied in a confident manly voice, "Hey."

"I'm Amber. What's your name?" She already knew his name, but she just wanted to start a conversation.

"I'm Jason. Nice to meet you."

Amber had to think of something quick before he walked right past her, "What's your favorite color?"

Jason stopped, "Green. What's yours?"

"Red."

He nodded, "Cool."

There was a pause. Amber asked, "So do you want to get something to eat?"

Jason shrugged and replied casually, "Sure."

* * *

Inside the little half-finished cottage, Mary finished putting supper on the kitchen table. It was a nice Southern meal the kids would be happy to come home from school and eat—plates of fried chicken, fried okra, corn, and mashed potatoes. Mary, John, and Will sat down at the table. They held hands, John said a blessing, and they started eating.

Will was the first to talk, "Mom."

Mary answered in her sweet voice, "Yes, darling?"

"I don't want to go to school anymore."

She put down her silverware, "Look, tomorrow I'm going to talk to the principle about Jimmy."

John finished chewing a bite, "And we'll make sure that none of this will ever happen again."

Will got a little choked up with emotion, "Okay." He was still petrified from the locker room situation.

Mary turned her attention to John, "So how was the meeting with the deacons today?"

John answered, "I can already tell that the deacons and I are not going to be very good friends. I met the assistant pastor, Chuck Freeman. Man, he's a real geek. He seems to think he owns the church."

Mary did not like what she had been dealing with for the past few weeks at all. She just remained silent.

John changed the subject, "Where's Amber?"

"She's out getting something to eat with a friend she met today at school."

John nodded, "Okay."

* * *

John's first official Sunday as pastor of the People of God was the same as the week before—the emotionless band singing and those in the crowd who were listening looking at him with eerily dispassionate stares. Assistant pastor Chuck Freeman sat in a chair next to John Benson and suspiciously eyed everything that he did. John did not like that man at all. Chuck was in his fifties with a baldhead, beady eyes, tight lips, and eyebrows that slanted downward. He was lanky and tall reaching 6'2, six inches taller than John. Having to literally look up to such a man made him feel even more uncomfortable.

John felt as dispassionate as his congregation and felt as if the oppressive atmosphere was sucking the life from him. As he had slowly walked to the podium, he had sighed an obvious heavy sigh before starting his well-prepared sermon. Of course, John knew that the sermon was just as spiritually dead as the crowd he was seeking to influence. But he also knew by his subtle grin that Chuck was enjoying his dead sermon.

Chuck wanted a dead sermon, because he enjoyed a dead church with brainwashed people. The more dead brainwashed people they had, the more stuff they bought from the gift shop. And the more they bought, the more money the church made, enabling Chuck to better satisfy his materialistic appetites. Yes, assistant pastor Chuck Freeman was very satisfied with a dead church, so Reverend Benson's dead sermon pleased him immensely.

As John preached, he couldn't help noticing that people in the pews were *talking*. And not only were they talking, some in the back were even standing, moving around and laughing, making it clear that they had no respect even for his position in the pulpit. John lowered his eyes to his notes in frustration. The people were acting as if John was not even there. In order to get through the sermon, he kept his eyes focused downward.

When he finished, he was forced to look up. As he observed his congregation, he was grateful that at least some were still staring at him, however dispassionately, but many were moving around and talking with other people as though he had never started preaching! John turned around and gave Chuck a confused look.

Chuck stood up from his chair and walked towards John, "Your time was up three minutes ago. You only have fifteen minutes and then it's over. These people have things to do and places to go."

A fury grew inside John, but he kept under control, "But what if I'm not finished yet?"

Chuck raised his voice and spoke forcefully, "But, you are, Reverend Benson."

John clenched his fists as he returned to his seat on the platform. Chuck was satisfied and stood to go as the band played a synthetic recessional. John was disturbed but relieved to be finished with his sermon.

Well at least I should talk with the people. John walked down the platform steps and into the crowd as they were lining up to file out of the sanctuary.

He caught one woman with two preschoolers and spoke in what he perceived as a friendly tone, "Hello, what's your name?"

The woman stopped and looked at him as if he was crazy, "Who are you?"

John pulled back offended. *Who am I?* He replied calmly, "I'm John Benson."

The woman still looked confused. "John Benson, John Benson," she repeated, "Aren't you the new pastor?"

John nodded, "Yes."

She nodded back, "Oh, okay. I got to go." Then she turned around and made her place in the line to exit.

John could only gaze in disbelief.

* * *

That night, John and Mary lay in bed talking with the bedside lamp still turned on.

John spoke, "I just don't get it. My church is dead. You saw how rude the crowd was and Chuck abruptly informed me that it was my fault for exceeding the sermon time limit. You know, after the service was over, when I went down to meet people, the first lady I spoke with didn't even know who I was. I told her my name and she still didn't know who I was.

"All Chuck cares about is money. All the deacons care about is money. The foundation of the church is money, not God. Yeah, we have over five thousand members, but

I don't think one of them, not *one* of them goes to the service thirsty for an encounter with God. I didn't sense God's presence at all.

"It appears that the goal of this church is to brainwash people. They come across as programmed zombies. They are programmed to walk into that sanctuary, sit down, and walk out buying stuff at the gift shop. It was an impersonal social hour. We do not have a church family at all. No one really knows anyone. Something's wrong." Suddenly, John stopped talking, his face contorted in pain, as he pressed his hand to his forehead.

Mary asked, "What's the matter, John?"

He face relaxed as the pain subsided, "I'm starting to get these weird headaches. Every day they get worse and worse. But they come and go so quickly."

"Maybe you should go see a doctor about it."

"I think I will." He released his hand from his forehead and continued, "Something's missing though. We have more money than we need, have all the music, all the equipment, all the special effects, and all the members we need to have a really great church."

Mary spoke, "What did do you in high school that made the Gathering a real revival for the kids at school?"

John shrugged, "I don't know."

Mary answered for him, "You took authority and gave the Holy Spirit complete control. You took charge and led people into the presence of God. You courageously obeyed God's call on your life and became a respected leader; you were the pastor of the gathering. So why can't you be the pastor of the People of God?"

"I am the pastor."

"Yes, but you're letting your church intimidate you."

John looked at Mary and the sparkle in his eye showed. And whenever Mary noticed the sparkle, she knew something was changing inside.

John turned on his side and mumbled in a tired voice, "I'm going to sleep. Goodnight."

"Goodnight." Mary turned off the lamp.

* * *

Whirling colored spotlights. 1964. Young high school band praising God with music. Hippies. Football players. Dorks. Old teachers. Young Mary in the crowd. Crying. Clapping. Hands up. Kneeling. Praising God. Worship. Heart. John. High school John. Skinny John. Bellbottoms. Wavy hair. Microphone.

"If you're here to goof off and hang out, then don't come!"

"...with every cell of muscle inside of you!"

Eight people in the library. 1,076 people in the gym.

"What about our popularity?"

"What about the law?"

"What about the money?"

"It'll never work."

More instruments. More singing. More people.

"Something that will never fail..."
Over a thousand people worshiping God.
"Something that will never fail is the..."
Audience listening carefully.
"The heart of worship!"

* * *

John woke up. It was dark and still in the bedroom. Mary was asleep. Now John was awake with those four words echoing in his mind—*the heart of worship.*

Chapter 4

The following Sunday Reverend John Benson walked into the People of God. Of course, no one noticed him, because they were too busy buying popcorn and coke, and shopping in the gift shop. As John walked past the entrance to the sanctuary, something caught his attention. A short, fat, female usher with curly hair was not letting an older man into the sanctuary. She had it roped off and stood in front of the rope. John walked towards them to better hear what was going on.

The usher repeated, "I'm sorry, sir. We cannot allow any more people to this service. But you can come to the 11:00 service and try again."

The old man replied in an uneasy voice, "But I want to hear what Christianity is all about. I've been Jewish all my life and I want to hear about Christianity."

"I'm sorry, sir."

Then the old man walked off toward the parking lot, as a new energy coursed through John's body. Energy he had not felt since he was in high school. His teenage power and authority was refueled. He seemed to have forgotten the rules of the People of God. He could let the church stay as it was or he could take his God-given responsibility seriously. He had the power to let the church be controlled by the Holy Spirit to the Glory of God or he could let it continue to be run by man.

John felt youthful strength return to his legs as he marched towards the usher.

The plump usher faced John and asked, "What can I do for you?"

"What were you thinking?" His voice was never harsh, but it was loud and stern when it needed to be. Some people turned to look at him.

The usher kept her stance, "What do you mean?"

John pointed his finger outside, "That man wanted to hear the Truth, and you just pushed him back out into darkness!"

"The People of God has certain rules and policies—"

"Forget about the rules and policies," John interrupted, "If this is the People of God, then let it be *His* church, not *your* church!"

"Sir, I'm just obeying the rules. If you have any complaints, then talk to the pastor about it."

"I *am* the pastor!"

She squinted her eyes, "So you are. I'm sorry, I didn't recognize you."

John shook his head in disbelief and said, "Just go home."

"Excuse me?"

"Go home. As long as you work in this church, you're here to help call people to Jesus, not push them back toward hell like you just did." With that, John walked off toward the platform door.

He sat down in his chair on the platform. Everything was agonizingly predictable. The band was getting ready, the thousands of people were sitting down, and Chuck sat in his seat next to John. The band was about to play when John stood up and motioned them to sit down. They obeyed and John made his way toward the microphone.

In a simple voice he spoke, "I have a few announcements to make." He faced the back of the sanctuary where the ushers were standing, "Ushers. One of you go and tell the gift shop and the concession stand to close and never open back up again."

The ushers stood in their places and looked at each other unsure what to do.

John urged, "Come on. You can do it. Tell all of them to shut down and get lost."

John just stood there waiting for one of them to do it. Finally, after hesitating uncomfortably for a few seconds, one of the ushers obeyed his request.

He continued, "No one is to be selling anything in this church ever again! Is that clear? Now all the technical crew up there, what's up with the cross buried behind all this jungle stuff? By next Sunday, I want either the cross to be moved in front of the jungle so it's more noticeable, or get rid of the jungle all together. One final announcement: I need to meet with the band real quick after the service.

He looked out at his congregation, "Now, how are you doing this morning?"

The people in the pews just stared at him.

"When someone asks you a question, it's always polite to answer."

A few nodded and others just mumbled a "good."

John smiled and clapped his hands once in excitement, "Good! That's the most active I've ever seen you! Now let's try the next step toward action. Who wants to come up here and give their testimony on how they met Jesus?"

Not a single person reacted.

John waited patiently, "Anyone?"

The only response was continued stares.

"Alright, you're too afraid to talk about Jesus. Let's tone it down a bit then. Everyone take out a piece of paper and a pen."

No one did. They weren't used to following direction and actually participating.

"Come on. It won't hurt you to take out a piece of paper and a pen."

Some of the people started taking out some paper and a pen, but others did not.

That was good enough. John continued, "Now all of you who have out a piece of paper and a pen, I want you to write a letter to Jesus."

Now, no one budged.

John raised his voice, "Come on. Forget you're in church right now!"

A few people looked down at the paper and started writing. John took his seat while these people wrote.

Chuck leaned over in his chair and attempting a forceful whisper, he half-yelled to John, "What is the meaning of this?"

John replied, "These people are spiritually dead. It's time for them to have a real conversation with Jesus."

"Well, you're scaring them half to death!"

John turned to face Chuck and spoke sternly, "If they are scared half to death to talk to Jesus, then something is seriously wrong here."

John heard a muffled whimper in the pews. He stood up and walked to the front of the platform. Right in the front row was a young man with a pen shaking in his hand as he held the point to the paper looking at his half-finished letter to Jesus. John walked down the steps towards the man.

As he saw John approach, he cleared his throat and tried to talk, "Reverend. I thought I was a Christian all my life. But I've just found out I can't even write a letter to Jesus. I was heading straight for hell all along!" The man leaped up from his chair and threw his arms around

John. John gladly hugged him back. The man started crying uncontrollably. Then he cleared his throat again, "Thank you for showing me the truth about myself."

* * *

"So where are you originally from?" Jason and Amber were walking side by side by themselves on the school campus during lunch on a nice sunny afternoon.

Amber answered, "A small town in Tennessee."

"Why'd you move down here?"

"My dad was asked to be pastor of a church here?"

"What church?"

"People of God."

Jason's thick eyebrows raised, "People of God?"

Amber nodded.

"Must be a pretty major preacher to be the pastor of that place."

She shrugged, "Yeah, I guess so. So what does your dad do?"

He exhaled, "He's a car mechanic. My mom's a housekeeper."

Amber nodded, "Cool. Well, we got to get to class. See ya." She waved with her fingers and walked toward her locker.

"See ya." Jason walked in the other direction.

Meagan and friends rushed towards Amber, "So you think you want to go out with him?"

Amber shrugged, "Maybe."

"You should. He's every girl's dream."

"Yeah, I know." Then they walked off chatting away.

*　　*　　*

It was one of Jason's good friends, Joe, who spotted Jason walking toward them. Joe shouted, "Hey man, I saw you hanging with that new Amber girl."

"She is one hot chick," Billy commented.

Jason smiled in delight, "She is pretty hot." He joined Billy and Joe in the little circle they always formed. They were all popular muscular guys. Jason's group and Meagan's group were the most popular groups in the eleventh grade.

Billy asked, "So are you going to hook up with her?"

Jason looked around to see if anyone was watching. Seeing no one, he stuck a cigarette between his lips, lit it with his lighter, inhaled, and breathed out gray smoke. He answered, "Maybe. I don't know, man. I need to test her out more. She may not be trashy enough for me. Her dad's the new pastor of People of God, so she might turn out to be too wholesome."

Joe and Billy lit a cigarette too. "Well, make her trashy," suggested Joe, "She has the body for it."

"You got that right," answered Jason.

*　　*　　*

The gray Volvo pulled into the elementary school, braking at the end of the pick-up line. Finally, he was next. One of the teachers opened the passenger door, "Name?"

John answered, "Will Benson."

She put the megaphone to her lips and shouted, "Will Benson."

John looked in the rearview mirror and saw his short skinny son looking at the ground with his hands in his pockets. He got in without saying a word. John pulled away from the curb and with a cheerful voice he asked, "So how was your day?"

Will looked up, "Terrible."

John kept his compassionate mood, "How was it terrible?"

"I still have no friends and everyone picks on me. The teachers say to just ignore them, but I want to stand up to them and start taking power."

John shook his head, "No, both of those are wrong. When I was your age, I had the same sort of problem. A lot of people picked on me, and I couldn't do anything about it because I was short and puny. So, then in high school, I wanted to change all that. That's when I started talking to the guys who picked on me. I started to become friends with them—"

Will gasped, "You became friends with the bad boys?"

"Well, not like best friends that I hung out with all the time. I also started talking to the athletic people, the drugged out hippies, and the dorks too and became friends with all of them. So I never became popular or a hippie or a dork or a bully. I started my own group, and through that group many students came to Christ."

"I wish I could do that."

"Sure you can. Just try and don't give up." John's hand went to his head in pain, "Ouch!"

Will panicked a little, "What's wrong?"

The pain went away as he lowered his hand back to the steering wheel, "I don't know. My headaches are getting worse every day."

* * *

Will picked up his tray of processed meat as his eyes skimmed the cafeteria for Jimmy's gang. There they were sitting over in the corner. They were easy to recognize. Instead of avoiding them and sitting in the opposite corner of the cafeteria, he walked right towards Jimmy's gang. It seemed to take forever to get over there, because he was so anxious. He came closer and closer until he could hear Jimmy's loud voice. Finally, he stood right in front of them with his tray in his hands.

Jimmy looked up. "What?" he demanded.

Will didn't answer, but sat down right next to him.

Jimmy's face twisted as he looked at his followers who also had twisted faces. Then he turned back to Will, "Weren't you supposed to stay away from us?"

Will looked up at him. "Hey, how's it going?" he said kindly as if he had been best friends with him all his life.

Jimmy answered shakily, unsure what had gotten into Will's head, "Good, I guess."

Will turned stiffly and nervously towards Jimmy, put his elbows on his legs, tilted his head and spoke, "So do you know Jesus?"

Jimmy was still confused but answered, "Yeah, of course I know who He is."

"No, do you personally *know* Him?"

Jimmy's defiant face softened, "Alright, who dared you to come over here?"

Will answered simply, "No one. I just wanted to know."

"What do you mean do I know Him?"

Will rephrased the question, "Are you a Christian?"

Jimmy was clearly bothered by the question. Shrugging, he muttered, "No."

"Well, being a Christian is pretty cool. I'm one. All it is, is when you let Jesus become your friend."

"Jesus is stupid."

"No he's not, he's awesome. Think about it. He was the Builder of the whole universe. And He created you and me and everyone else in this world."

Jimmy had had a question on his mind all his life that he had never asked until now, "Then why isn't the world perfect?"

"Because of our sinful nature."

"Nature?"

"Character."

"Okay, whatever. Then why do we have a sinful character?"

Will leaned in closer to Jimmy and spoke more quietly, "Because when the Devil told humans to sin, we fell for it. And all the sin we did built a barrier made of sin that broke us away from God. And because God loved us and cared for us so much, he sent His Son down to earth and put Him into a man's body and he was named Jesus. But we were so sinful that we killed Him and nailed him on the barrier made of sin. Can you believe it? I mean we actually nailed God to our sinful barrier. Well it turned out that Jesus died on that barrier."

"So why is He so awesome?"

"I'm not finished yet. Anyway, after He died, he came back to life. For real, He came back to life. And when He came back to life, guess what happened? That big barrier made of our sin that separated us from God was broken. Well, Jesus went to heaven and He's still there. But He did send someone to earth called the Holy Spirit to be with us. All of us build our own sinful barriers, but if we just let Jesus be our friend and give our whole life to Him, then He will break that barrier for you so that you can have a relationship with God. It's as simple as that."

Jimmy was too big and tough to react positively in front of his gang, but Will could see something happening to him. His hands were fidgeting as if he was scared. Jimmy's voice was even quivering as he spoke, "Get out of here."

Will knew what that meant. He quickly picked up his tray and walked away from that table. He hoped that he did not make Jimmy hate him even more now. At least new thoughts were planted in his mind. Will walked off and found some other table to sit at.

Never before in his life had he felt this confident. Yes, he inherited a lot from his father—his body, his looks. But there was something else he inherited from his father, and that was his passion to serve God.

Chapter 5

Mary was washing dishes in the sink because the dishwasher wasn't installed yet. She wore an apron as she looked out the window at her newly planted garden. The afternoon sun reflected off the beads of water on the flowers she had just watered.

She heard the creaky spring door open and slam shut and hollered, "What'd the doctor say?"

John entered the kitchen, "He said that it is most likely migraine headaches caused by too much stress and traveling. He gave me some pills to take."

"So it's nothing major?"

"He doesn't think so, but he said to get a CT scan." He puffed out the words half-laughing, "I don't know if I can afford that."

Mary turned from the sink and dried her hands on a towel, "Honey, you're going to have to get that checked out."

"Okay, I will."

*   *   *

"How many of you believe in demons?" It was the 11:00 Sunday service at the People of God. The gift shop was closed, the popcorn stand was closed, the cross was moved more in the center and in front of the jungle, and the crowd wasn't as big as it usually was today. Chuck Freeman sat in his chair monitoring John as usual, becoming more suspicious.

John continued, "I don't believe in them."

No reaction.

"Come on, who believes in demons?"

The crowd just stared at him.

John raised his voice, "Are you listening? I just said something totally false and all you can do is stare?"

The crowd started looking at each other.

John continued, "There *are* such things as demons! This church is full of them." John raised his voice almost yelling, "Full of them! In fact, the biggest, most vicious demon I see here is named 'Do anything to get money.'" John twisted his body to face Chuck, "Isn't that right?" He turned back around to the congregation. "There's another demon named, 'I'm not going to listen to a single word the preacher has to say.' Hello? Are you listening? Know what? I see thousands of slobbery demons right now hopping from shoulder to shoulder making you think about something else other than the sermon. So right now, I want all of you to look at your shoulder and shout out, 'Demon! In Jesus' name, I command you to leave me right now!'"

No one did anything.

John raised his eyebrows and tapped the podium with his fingers, "I'm waiting."

Some people started mumbling the phrase.

John spoke, "That's not going to do it. Come on. Shout it out! Make those demons hear you! Jesus is giving you power over them, so use it! With all your strength, with all you're worth, command those little demons! Forget that you're in church; forget that you might embarrass yourself! Right now, there is no one in this room except for you and Jesus versus Satan! Whip those little slimy demons back into place! Strengthen the angels with the authority Jesus has given to you!" John took a deep breath and shouted as loud as he could, "Satan! In Jesus' name, I command you to leave this sanctuary right now!"

Suddenly, the crowd became energized. Not all, but many of the people began shouting, commanding the demons to leave them right then in Jesus' name. Most of the people in the back just sat there confused. Still many people in the front row were becoming increasingly loud, more physical, and more aggressive. Soon the sanctuary was filled with shouting.

Chuck Freeman sat there appalled and disgusted. His fists clinched with anger as he got up and marched to the podium. He shoved John away and put his lips on the microphone yelling, "Alright, that's enough!"

The crowd immediately fell silent and looked up at the well-known bald assistant pastor of the church.

Chuck yelled, "We are in church, not at a playground! We cannot allow all this noise and this absurd yelling!"

John was about to step in until Chuck yelled, "Reverend Benson, meet me in my office!"

John opened his mouth about to say something—

"Now!"

John closed it and headed out the platform door.

Chuck lowered his voice a little, "This service is over."

* * *

"What was that?" exclaimed Chuck as flying spit landed on John's face. Chuck's office was a nice one. The walls were covered with genuine cherry wood and so was his desk. An antique grandfather clock made the only background sounds.

John said calmly, "Ordering Satan out of the church."

Chuck took off his glasses and held out his finger, "First of all, Satan is not in the church. Second, you are supposed to preach, not perform exorcism. And finally, all that noise and commotion was completely uncalled for."

John looked at him straightforwardly, "I'm just doing what's right." He had not spoken those words in a long time.

Chuck replied, “No, you’re doing the opposite. You better get polished up. We do have deacons, and the deacons do have power over you so you better watch yourself and get it under control.”

John stood, “What do you mean ‘get it under control’? I do what’s right! I do what God wants me to do! And I’m not going to let you or anyone change that! Do you understand me?”

Chuck gave an attitude back, “I’m not saying to stop doing the Lord’s will. I’m just saying get it under control and—“

“And preach dead sermons?” John interrupted, “Preach dead sermons?”

Chuck did not answer.

“Is that what you want me to do? Make sure this church is dead? Keep the members dead? Brainwash them with the love of money?”

Chuck swallowed. He couldn’t answer that question so he said, “You’re dismissed Reverend Benson.”

John gave him another piercing gaze and walked out of the office.

* * *

Ring! The telephone rang. Mary placed the stirring spoon beside the stove and put the receiver to her ear, “Hello? Just one moment please.” She placed the phone on the table and called down the hallway, “Amber, telephone!”

Amber quickly walked to the kitchen and picked it up, "Hello?"

A guy's voice was on the other end, "Hey, this is Jason."

She smiled with delight, "Oh, hey."

"Do you have any plans this Friday night?"

Her heart started beating with excitement, but she tried to maintain a controlled voice, "No."

"Do you want to go out with me?"

Now her heart was really beating, "Sure."

"Okay. I'll pick you up at 6:00. Does that sound good?"

"Sure."

"Okay. Bye."

"Bye."

Amber hung up the telephone. Mary was concentrating on her food preparations. Without looking up she asked, "Who was it?"

Amber answered, "Mom. I'm going on a date on Friday."

* * *

Billy jumped on the bed Jason was sitting on eager to know, "What'd she say?"

Jason smirked, "She said yes."

Billy laughed.

Joe was sitting on the other bed. He joked, "You player." All three of them were in their boxers with empty cans of coke lying on the floor and cigarette smoke fogging up the bedroom.

Jason reminded his buds, "Remember I'm only doing this to test her out. Hey Billy, where'd you put the beer?"

Joe leaped off the bed, walked to the closet, and opened the door revealing several six-packs of beer.

Joe commented, "In the closet, how original."

"Well, my parents never come in my room anyway."

Jason tossed his cigarette out the window, "All right guys, let's drink."

*   *   *

John threw on a white smock. The room was all white. There must have been a reason for that. Right beside him was a big white machine with a narrow metal bed, obviously a place to lie down on in order to go head first into the opening of the space age machine.

The nurse spoke, "We will do two tests. The first one will be the computerized topography scan and the other will be the magnetic resonance imaging scan. This will give us a thorough view of your brain. Okay?"

John nodded, "Okay."

The nurse smiled, "Okay, lay down on your back with your head at this end."

He did so. The nurse strapped his head and reminded him, "It's important that you don't move at all during this. I'll be out of the room." With that said, she closed the door and the humming of the CT machine started. John felt the metal table roll back into the machine. He found the distractions inside the machine nice actually. Lights rotated around him for a while. He prayed. *Please Lord. Don't let this be serious.* Finally, the lights stopped and he rolled back out. The humming stopped.

* * *

It was lunchtime again in the elementary school. Will picked up his tray and walked into the cafeteria.

"Hey Will!"

A familiar voice came from next to him. He turned and saw Jimmy's gang sitting down eating. Jimmy pulled out a chair next to him, "Have a seat. We want to hear more about this Jesus thing."

A smile appeared on Will's face as he sat down.

* * *

John sat in the waiting room. He was waiting there for a very long time, and the longer he waited the more nervous he became. What if he did have a tumor? What if they couldn't remove it? What if it was cancerous? What if it was deadly? What would happen to the church? What would happen to his family? Oh, stop worrying!

Suddenly, the door opened and jarred him from his dark thoughts. A young doctor approached him and spoke in a low voice, "Mr. Benson. I'm afraid we have some bad news." She switched on a light inside a panel and clipped x-rays over it. John stood next to her as she explained the picture of John's multi-colored brain.

The doctor pointed to an orange spot in the middle of the brain, "Here is the source of your headaches."

John's eyes widened, "Is that a tumor?"

She nodded sympathetically and continued, "This particular tumor is what we call a glioblastoma multiforme. These type of tumors are too deep in the brain to remove."

John became terrified, and his voice was barely audible, "So what are you going to do about it? Is it cancerous?"

She nodded, "Yes, it's brain cancer, and we have no cure for this kind of cancer. We will give you special drugs to relieve the pain, control seizures, reduce brain swelling, and hopefully slow the growth, but, like I said, the tumor you have is inoperable."

Tears formed in John's trusting eyes and his lip quivered with emotion, "But there's still a chance that you can cure it?"

"I'm sorry."

Chapter 6

"So are you a Christian?" It was Friday night at about 11:00. Jason was driving Amber home from the date in his very old rusty Mercury Cougar.

Amber answered sheepishly, "Yeah. Are you?"

Jason answered casually, "Nope. Too many rules and boundaries for me. I like to have a little fun in my life."

"Well, you can still have fun when you're a Christian, you just have to obey God's law."

"But your dad's a pastor, so you won't be able to have any fun."

She nodded, "And he doesn't even father me. He doesn't even love me it seems. He's so out of my life that he probably doesn't even know that I'm gone right now."

Jason's voice grew quiet and comforting, "Hey, that's why I'm here for you. And I will always be here for you." It was all a lie. An act he put on to get what he wanted.

* * *

Across from the Bensons' cottage, a bush shook. Squatting behind it were Joe and Billy waiting for the Mercury Cougar to pull up.

Joe whispered, "How far do you think they went?"

Billy whispered back, "Probably not even to first. Jason is testing, remember?"

"Yeah—" He stopped short when they both heard a car approaching. The headlights came into view, as a Mercury Cougar squealed to a stop in front of the cottage. They watched through the bushes. The passenger door opened and Amber stepped out and walked to the front step of the doorway. She stopped and turned around to look at Jason who was still sitting in the car watching her. He smiled and waved and she waved back, as she went inside and shut the door.

Joe and Billy leaped out of the bushes still cautiously squatting as they walked to the passenger door. They opened it, piled in, and Jason drove off.

Joe was the first to talk, "So how'd it go?"

Jason answered, "Just how I expected it to go."

Billy spoke, "Do you think you can make her trashy?"

Jason smirked, "I don't think I'll have any problem. She'll do anything for me."

*　*　*

The next Sunday, even fewer people showed up at the People of God. The top two balconies were completely empty, the band wasn't playing, the gift shop remained closed, and not a single person gave money to the church. The church's income was zero.

John walked up to the podium and spoke, "So I see that we have fewer people than we usually do. Man, the first day I came here, every seat was full. Now the top two balconies are empty. Wow, in just a couple months. But why are they leaving? The answer is very simple. Listen closely," John leaned in and spoke very clearly, "They are not serious about their faith. And what are they missing? The heart of worship. I'm telling you right now, if you don't want to worship God, you don't even need to be here. If you are worried about being late for a party or a sporting event or dinner because of church, then don't even bother to come." He assessed the crowd, and for the first time, not all, but some were actually listening. Still, most were just staring.

John moved to the front of the platform talking specifically to the people in the back who just stared, "Some of you are just staring at me like I'm crazy. I don't know why you're here! Those of you who are listening and wanting more, God bless you!"

He searched the faces of the crowd once more and then said, "I think we need to pray right now." John closed his eyes, "Dear Lord. Please Lord, this church *needs* you. We are thirsty for you. Restore Your church and make us holy. Help us come back to the heart of worship where You are all we seek.

Help us see that You are what this church really needs and that You are looking for worshipers who will worship in Spirit and in Truth." Chuck was scowling as John concluded, "In Jesus' name we pray, Amen."

*   *   *

Mary had just finished saying goodnight to Will and was wiping the kitchen counters. John walked downstairs and Mary heard him get his keys off the key rack. She glanced up at him, "Where are you going at this hour? And what are you wearing?"

John was dressed in holey blue jeans and a holey tee shirt he had not worn in years. He replied simply, "I'm going downtown."

She stopped the sink and questioned him wide-eyed, "Downtown? Why?"

He shrugged, "God is telling me to go." He started making his way to the door.

"Wait, how do I know you're safe?"

He shouted behind him, "Pray." With that, he slammed the door and made his way to his car.

John traveled down the expressway. Millions of white headlights zoomed to the left. It was quite a spectacular sight. The traffic slowed as he made his way into downtown Atlanta. It was bigger than he realized. The tall buildings were clustered together just like in pictures, but as he came closer and closer and the skyscrapers became taller and taller, the buildings towering over his car made him feel so small. The fantastic light of the city combined with the spaghetti-like bridges of different highways looping around and above him created a dizzying sensation. When he saw the Atlanta Braves' baseball stadium, Turner Field, John laughed aloud at his country boy roots. He had never been out of his small Tennessee town until now, and so this big city was overwhelming for him.

As he drove further into the city, the glamour vanished and was replaced by abandoned buildings and factories. As John exited, it was dark and he saw no moving cars down the lonely side street. As he drove deeper into the darkness, stray dogs were the first life to greet him. Then, he noticed mostly black homeless people pushing grocery carts full of what looked like trash. As John came upon an especially dark and desolate back alley, he parked the car.

* * *

Mary opened the bathroom door. John's prescription pills for his headaches were opened by the sink, as if he were in a hurry before he left to go downtown. What was he taking anyway? She picked up the three bottles of pills and read the labels. The first one: analgesics. The second one: anticonvulsants. And the third one: corticosteroids. She gasped. These were no normal headache pills. These indicated something more serious than simple headaches.

* * *

John walked confidently, bravely through the dark alley and out onto a street where he could hear dogs barking, prostitutes laughing, children screaming, and men shouting all around him. He turned into an alley with a strong aroma of marijuana in the air. Young, gaunt, black men with swollen watery eyes passed by looking at him strangely. He walked on. A black man sitting with his back against the wall caught his eye. He was obviously selling marijuana and other drugs. John stepped closer to him until he was standing right in front of him.

The man looked at him, "This is our 'hood," he mumbled. The man looked to be in his fifties with gray curly hair. Most of his teeth were gone and the remaining teeth were decayed and mostly black. He was smoking pipe, obviously not tobacco, and had a foul stench about him.

John sat down next to him and replied calmly, "Who says?"

The drug dealer stared at him, "Boy, you lookin' for trouble?"

John shook his head, "No."

"You came here to buy? 'Cuz I don't sell to your kinda white trash."

"I'm not here to buy." John decided to get to the point, "Why do you sell drugs?"

"Boy, you cop or sum'?"

"No, I'm not a cop. Why do you sell drugs?" John repeated.

"I don't know why I sells drugs. Just a hobby."

"I mean... there must be some reason why you do drugs. I don't think you woke up one day and said, 'I'm going to become addicted to drugs today.'"

"Cuz they makes me feel good. Wuss your pro'm with 'em?"

"Sure, they make you feel good. But why do you need to feel good? Why don't you already feel good?"

He raised his voice a little, "Boy, that's my biz'ness!"

"You're trying to fill an empty space, a void deep inside you. You've probably tried every drug out there to fill that void. Sure, drugs can numb the void, but it's still there. But I know something that can fill that void."

"What?"

"Jesus. Ever heard of Jesus?"

The man shook his head, "No, never heard of Jesus."

"This Sunday I want to show you Jesus. Early Sunday morning, I will drive down here in a bus to pick you and your other drug dealers and customers up and show you Jesus."

He nodded, "I'll do it. Now this better not be some kind of joke," he warned.

John had to laugh, "Don't worry, this isn't a joke. What's your name by the way?"

The man answered, "Ernie."

John stuck out his hand, "Nice to meet you Ernie."

Ernie hesitated for a second and studied John's hand as if it was poisonous. Then, very cautiously he stuck out his dry, bony, hand and shook John's.

John stood and walked out of the alley. He looked up. The skies were dark and cloudy and with the ambient light of the city, no light of moon or star shown. Just across the street, he saw a group of young women. Some were gaunt-looking and some were fat, but they were all dressed the same. In the distance, John could make out a bearded dirty man placing money into one of the women's hands, as they walked off down the street. It was clear that he was in the red-light district. Prostitutes surrounded him.

One of the bony hookers noticed him walking eagerly towards them so she spoke softly, "Looks like another customer." The other women looked up and saw him too.

"A good-looking one too," one said, "We don't get too many of those around." The others agreed.

A chunky woman stepped out and greeted him, "Hey cutie."

John replied, "Hey." Then he stopped right in front of them, "Can I ask you a question?"

"We're open," one answered.

He continued, "Why do you sell yourselves as prostitutes?"

They glanced at each other uneasily. No customer ever asked that question before. The chunky one answered, "Quick, easy money. That's all what it's about honey."

John nodded and lowered his eyebrows as if he was thinking hard, "It is quick. But why is it easy?"

Now all the women traded glances, hoping someone would come up with something. Was he just stupid or something? The chunky one answered again, "What do you mean how is it easy? You are paid for getting laid. How easy is that?"

"Pretty easy," John sat down. "But you're still selling your bodies. Don't you ever get this dirty, disgusting feeling? And don't you ever get this voice inside of you condemning you and saying, 'you're repulsive?'"

This time, the chunky woman did not come up with an immediate answer. She thought for a moment and then answered, "That's just our life."

"Would you want to change that?"

Her answer was casual and careless, "Can't."

"Actually, you can."

She looked up at him, "What are you trying to pull?"

"Nothing. I'm just saying that there is a hope. And that hope can give you all the money you'll ever need."

"What are you talking about?"

He smiled, “Early Sunday morning, I’ll be here in a big bus to pick up some homeless people, and some drug dealers, and all of you. From there, I’ll show you the hope I’m talking about.”

The chunky woman looked away and shook her head, “Okay, whatever you say.”

“See ya then.” With that, John walked back to his Volvo while the prostitutes and the drug dealers continued to do their work.

*   *   *

John flung open the cottage door and saw Mary sitting on the couch. He started talking immediately, “Man, this is so awesome! I met with drug dealers and a bunch of prostitutes, and on Sunday I’m—“ He stopped short. Mary’s face showed that she was clearly upset. He asked, “What’s wrong?”

She answered, “Your headaches are not just from anxiety.”

John took a deep breath and exhaled rubbing his eyes. He sat down on the couch next to Mary and put his arm around her. He spoke as lovingly as he could, “You’re not going to like this.”

“I know I’m not.”

“Well, I got my CT scan yesterday. And the reason I haven’t told you about it yet is because I got home late last night and you were already asleep, and today we went to church and I was working all afternoon. But, I'll tell you now. The doctor studied the pictures of my brain." He paused. "Let me put it bluntly." He took another deep breath, "I have brain cancer."

Mary's eyes widened as she turned to face him, "Brain cancer?"

He nodded.

She groped for words, "Well-well, can they fix it?"

He spoke very slowly and very clearly, "You can't cure this kind of cancer. The object is to get rid of the brain tumor. But the problem with my tumor is that it's so deep and large, they can't surgically remove it. So now, I'm on drugs to shrink the tumor and to help with the pain. The third drug keeps me from having side effects like seizures and that kind of stuff."

Mary couldn't say anything. Overwhelmed with all this information, she fell into John's arms and grasped his shirt shedding tears. John held her and whispered comforting words into her ear.

*   *   *

VROOM. The nice, white, clean, brand-new People of God bus sped across the ghetto. The driver was John dressed in a coat and tie ready for church. The alleys looked the same as before, but he felt more comfortable this time, as the light of the new day was dawning. John looked up at the early morning sun slowly popping above the orange and pink clouds shining its light against the dirty, concrete, abandoned buildings. He could sense hope in this ghetto. He could sense a special thirstiness.

He arrived at the dark, dirty alley, much lighter now. He slammed on his brakes. He did tell Ernie to bring along some of his partners, but he did not expect him to bring this many. Crowds of gaunt, scrappy, mostly black men who looked similar to Ernie immediately pushed their way towards the bus door. John pulled the lever and the door opened as the eager drug addicts and dealers piled in. A whiff of the rotten smell of the alley blew in. Each man who walked in smiled at John who smiled back. They made their way to the back of the bus and filled most of the seats. The last man who came in was Ernie. Through the drunken, wasted, and pitiful face, a smile broke through.

John smiled back, "I promise you'll like it."

Ernie's smile grew bigger, "Got a feelin' I will." Then he took a seat. The disheveled men looked around the bus and marveled at the luxury. John closed the door and pressed the gas pedal. He did a U-turn and went a short distance, slamming on his brakes again on the opposite side of the street.

Three times as many prostitutes as John saw before appeared from an alley looking more disgusting in the daylight than they did at nighttime. They crowded around the bus door and John flung it open. Now the prostitutes came in, each hoping John would notice her.

He yelled to the back, "Guys, make room for the ladies!"

They obeyed and started fitting three or four to a seat. Some stood up. As the prostitutes moved through the bus, the men started whooping and whistling at them.

John yelled back, "Keep it calm back there!"

They quieted down. John closed the doors. Now it was very crowded. Everyone squeezed in, some sitting, some standing. There were a good sixty people in that bus. John knew that none of these people ever heard of Jesus. But all of them wanted to know Him.

*   *   *

Chuck checked his watch. 9:17. Reverend Benson was seventeen minutes late. The pews were less populated than ever. The people were sparsely scattered through half of the bottom section. Only a few hundred came this Sunday. The band had quit, as they weren't being paid, so there was no music. The gift shop was closed, so no money was being made. No people. No music. No money. No pastor. No people. No music. No money. No pastor. Chuck's palms sweated against the wood of his chair as he gripped it tightly. There was definitely going to be a deacon's meeting tonight.

Suddenly, the back door flew open. John walked in quickly down the aisle. Following him were twenty inner-city drug dealers and forty prostitutes. Chuck sprung from his chair with his eyes bulging. Sixty homeless city scums were invading the People of God. Many members got up and walked out disgusted leaving about eighty members there with sixty homeless people. Chuck clenched his fists.

John led the prostitutes and drug dealers to pews and quickly walked up on the platform. Chuck said sternly, "Are you out of your mind? What do you think you're doing?"

John dropped his shoulders and asked, "What do you *think* I'm doing?"

"You're filling this church with dangerous—"

"I'm the pastor of this church and I take responsibility for the visitors I have brought today."

"But you can't—"

"Do you have a problem with me preaching the gospel to these people?"

"Well, no, but—"

"Then sit down and pray!"

Chuck's mouth shut. He could tell by the seriousness in John's eyes that he was not joking. He sat down.

John walked to the podium and looked specifically at his visitors. Mary and Will sat in the pews, but Amber was out "doing her own thing."

He began, "Before life, before this world, before the entire universe, and before the atom, what was there? Was there nothing? There had to be something in order to trigger off whatever started us. There had to be some source that generated life. Right?"

The visitors thought about that and then slowly nodded.

"Right. But what *was* the source that generated life? What generated everything? You know, for many years now, the world's smartest guys have been wondering that themselves. So, after years of studying and experimenting, they finally came up with a theory that is taught at all the public schools in America. And do you want to know what that theory is that these smart people came up with? The source that generated life was absolutely nothing. Absolutely nothing. All of the sudden out of nowhere BOOM! Everything was made right then. That's the theory!"

The visitors actually started laughing. They thought the theory was absolutely ridiculous. Even John started laughing. It *was* a ridiculous theory.

John continued, "Isn't that stupid?" Then he grew very serious and the visitors quieted down, "I got a secret that those smart people don't know. Want to hear it?"

The visitors shouted, "Yeah!"

"Alright, I'll tell you. I know how everything was *really* made. Before anything began, all there was—was something called the spiritual realm. But we don't fully comprehend the spiritual realm because our human minds can't grasp it all. In the spiritual realm, there existed big powerful God. He was the God of everything.

He owned all the nothingness around him. Since He owned the nothingness, he could do anything He wanted to do with it. So that's when He created the stars, the moon, the sun, the planets, His beautiful home called heaven, and the skies.

"Then, He created a special planet called Earth by creating the oceans, then the land, then all the vegetation, and then the fish and animals and birds. God really liked His creation. That's when He said, 'I want to make something special. Something unique. Something that has a Spirit to worship Me.' That's when He created man."

John could tell that his visitors were listening.

He continued, "Now this man couldn't see God or physically hear him or touch him. Do you know why? Because God was still in the spiritual realm and this man was in the human realm. And in the human realm, your human eyes can't see what goes on in the spiritual realm and you can't hear or touch the spiritual realm. However, we humans do have a way to connect with the spiritual realm. God gave man His image and placed His Spirit within us. So, God talked to this man all the time. And this man listened all the time. How? By God's Spirit. I know it's hard to get, but that's just because our brains are so stupid when it comes to this spiritual stuff. God saw that it was not good for the man to be alone, so God made a female partner for him."

The drug dealers started whooping and whistling. At least they were listening.

"And this man and this lady went together perfectly. I mean, they were a perfect match. Since this man had never seen a woman before, God had to give instructions. He said, 'This is your mate. This is your special partner. And because this is your special partner, she is called your wife. And you and your wife can have sex all you want to and reproduce and populate the world.'" He was looking specifically at the prostitutes who were growing uncomfortable.

John's tone changed, "Now let's fast-forward in time a little bit. That man and woman did reproduce, and over time, the whole world was populated with people. We found out how to build cities and how to make clothes. We were so caught up with ourselves that we forgot about God. He tried to talk to us but we were so busy and so distracted with ourselves that we didn't listen. We started doing things that pleased ourselves that was totally opposite of what God wanted us to do. There's a special word for that. It's called sin. Sin took over our lives. And God *hates* sin, but he *loved* us! It was so frustrating to Him because He loved us so much, but He couldn't *get* to us because we were absolutely covered and buried with sin. And in the spiritual realm, sin was very clear and very visible to see. Sin is like the nastiest growing mold in the spiritual realm. But we humans couldn't see it, couldn't understand the sin that was growing on us because still our minds have a hard time thinking in spiritual terms.

"I know this is weird to understand, although God is one being, He is three persons—the Father, the Son, and the Holy Spirit. The Son said to His Father, 'Dad, I am going to leave this glorious perfect heaven, and I am going to become a man, live down on Earth with all that sin, so that I can break through the barrier it has made.' So, that's what happened. A normal teenaged lady gave birth to God's Son who looked just like a man, had the same feelings and emotions like a man, but He was God. His name was Jesus."

The drug dealers looked at each other and were surprised. Is this the new drug this man was talking about?

John raised his voice, "Do you think Jesus was the most popular king of the world? Do you think all the earthly kings bowed down and worshipped him? No! I mean here's God on earth trying to scrape away the sinful mold on us, and we were so stupid, so mindless, so blind, and so sinful that we killed him. Do you know how we killed him? We literally nailed him to a wooden cross that was about six feet tall. Pure torture. Why did we kill him? He didn't do anything wrong so why did we kill him? It was because we couldn't help ourselves. With our sinful nature controlling our lives, we killed Him! When Jesus was nailed to the cross, he was tortured not only by the physical pain, but also the spiritual pain. He was still God, so he was even more tortured by all of our sin upon Him. All of the sin that was in the world was smothering Him at that moment. We can't really understand that because again our minds are set to think logically, not spiritually. In fact, Jesus was smothered with so much sin that, in the spiritual realm, even God, the Father, turned His face away from Him because He was so disgusting looking with the sinful scum.

"Finally, Jesus' body died," he lowered his voice to a very quiet clear voice, "Then do you know what happened three days later, as He lay in a tomb? Jesus came back to life! He was resurrected from the dead! Why? Because, we can't kill God. You can kill a man's body, but you can't kill God. And at that moment, sin and death were conquered. Jesus went back to heaven to be with His Father again where He belongs, but this time, all the sin was cleared away, allowing us to have a relationship with God Himself. Now that is true love!

"We all, every single person in this room, are covered with sin, including me. Yes, I still sin. But I gave my life to Jesus when I was young. And if we truly ask for forgiveness for all of our sins, it doesn't matter how bad it is, He will forgive us and totally trash that sin forever! We will still sin sometimes, but Jesus is willing to take all that sin for you, because He loves all of you. He wants you to dump all your sin at the cross. He wants a relationship with every single one of you! If you would only give your sin and your life to Jesus, you can have a personal and special relationship with God Himself. He still is there and He hasn't changed since He created the universe. He loves each and every one of you so much that he knows all of your names, everything you ever said in your life, and He even knows you better than you know yourself. He even knows the exact number of hairs you have. Why? Because He created you. You are His Creation. If you would give your whole entire life to Jesus, you will have a relationship unlike any relationship you ever had before. In that relationship, you will be able to live in heaven with God forever! Jesus doesn't come in pill form. You don't have to inhale Him every day to get high on Him. Remember He's still in the spiritual realm so you have to do things spiritually. How do you get high on Jesus? You just simply ask him to forgive you and give you His power to live the life that God intends for you to live. You just ask him. He can hear you. Just ask him to totally take over your life and transform it. I promise He won't let you down. He *will* fill that emptiness inside of you. He *will* give you a hope. He *will* give your life meaning. You're not worthless in His eyes. Underneath all that sin, He still loves you. In fact, whenever any person gives his life to Jesus, God throws a big party up in heaven. I'm not making this up. This is not some kind of myth. This is the truth. You can ask anyone who knows Him; Jesus really does exist. And He really is the Son of God. All this is in this book right here." He held up his leather Bible. "And this famous book has all the answers you need to life. Do it. Get high on Jesus. He will save you."

Immediately drug addicts, dealers and prostitutes rushed up to the platform. Chuck cringed. "Tell me more, tell me more," they shouted. John smiled. They were starving, eager for Jesus. Suddenly, a strong hand landed on John's shoulder. He stood up and turned around. He was facing Ernie who still had that wasted appearance when he spoke, "Boy, give me some of that Jesus."

John extended his heavy Bible to him, "Take this."

Ernie grinned, revealing his black teeth, took the Bible from John's hand, and spoke in a gentler voice, "Thank you. You keeps up your teachings now."

John smiled a little, "My life would be pointless if I didn't." His eyes narrowed like they always did when he was serious, and he put his hands on Ernie's bony shoulders, "Ernie, I want you to take that book and start getting high on Jesus. It's very important that you do that. Share with all your friends about Him. Okay?"

Ernie nodded slowly, "Of course I will."

John smiled and wrapped his arms around Ernie. Ernie hugged him tighter as John spoke, "Ernie, you're a good man. Make a difference where you live. In your 'hood."

Ernie replied, "I will, I will." Then he let go of John and walked back towards his partners with John's Bible in his hand.

Chapter 7

John opened the door and stepped inside the conference room. Inside, the Board of Deacons was seated around a huge cherry wood table. All of them were very professional looking, wearing coats and ties, many in glasses, and all with carefully groomed hair. At the head of the table sat the lanky bald Chuck Freeman. "Have a seat," he said coldly.

John pulled out the only empty chair facing Chuck. He sat down. Chuck leaned forward on his elbows and looked directly at John, "Reverend Benson, we have met to discuss a very serious matter. The Board of Deacons and I are very concerned with the direction the church is going in. We have been one of the largest churches in the southeast for a long time now. My father paid for this magnificent facility, and he expects me to be here making sure that his wishes are carried out. Reverend Johnson was the pastor here for seven years. In those seven years, we had a huge increase in membership and profit. We sent him to establish a new work in a similar community. He promised us that he would find us a great pastor to enable this church to continue to grow. We trusted him, and he found you. Therefore, we have been giving you chance after chance to help this church grow. However, we have experienced the opposite. The income of the church is as low as it has ever been. We feel like we have good reason to believe that you are behind all this corruption." Chuck nodded at one of the deacons, "Ed, show Reverend Benson our financial progress."

A heavy man with a deep voice stood and walked over to the dry-erase board pulling down a chart over it, "Reverend Benson, this chart indicates the progress of the church's income." It was a line chart with a red line going almost straight down. "As you can see, our income has dropped dramatically since Reverend Johnson left. The day he left, this church was worth approximately thirty million dollars, not only from gift shop sales, but also from government and corporate sponsorship of social programs. Unfortunately, when you ordered all sales to terminate, the government and corporations weren't interested in funding us anymore and our income plummeted."

John asked, "Then why didn't the members help support the church?"

Ed struggled for an answer, "Well…because—"

Chuck answered for him, "Because we're not that kind of church here. We don't want to scare and pressure our members to give money out of obligation."

Ed nodded in agreement, "That's right."

John asked, "So your goal is not to pressure the members to give money to the church out of obligation, but to obtain money through merchandising, taxes, and advertising for corporations. Right?"

Chuck answered, "Right, it's the American way."

John mumbled to himself, "American way."

"Excuse me?"

"Nothing. And why do we need money?"

Chuck answered, "To make this church grow."

"But why does it need to grow?"

"To attract people."

John's voice rose a little, "How can money attract people?"

Chuck was becoming a bit irritated, "By enhancing worship."

"Enhancing the worship with money? That's the most—" He stopped himself. He knew he could not explode right in a deacon's meeting.

Chuck turned to Ed, "You may be seated."

* * *

Inside of the Bensons' cottage, Jason and Amber sat close together on the couch. No one was in the room except them, the only light was coming from a lamp, and they were serenaded by the soft sound of crickets chirping outside. How peaceful.

Amber sat there with thoughts flowing in her head. *Out of all the girls in the school, why me?* That was the most common thought.

"I think you're the most awesome girl in the school."

Amber looked up into his eyes, "Do you really mean that or are you just saying that to make me feel better?"

He raised one side of his mouth, "Of course I mean that. Do you think I would lie to you?"

She did not answer because she felt the back of her hand rub against his. Like a magnet, the palms of their hands came together as they intertwined fingers. She looked up in his eyes as he looked back. For a moment, they just gazed. Slowly their heads moved closer to each other, as they embraced.

* * *

"Another issue I would like to point out," continued Chuck, "is when you caused all that noise during the service."

John looked at him, "Noise?"

"When you encouraged our members to start screaming at demons."

"They weren't just screaming at demons. They were commanding them to leave this church."

"There aren't any demons in this church. This is the People of God, not the Church of Demons. I believe in rebuking demons, but doing it in a noisy fashion is not appropriate for this church." He looked at John, waiting for a reply.

John did so respectfully, "Yes, sir."

"Good. One very important issue we need to discuss is what occurred this morning. First, you spoke to me very disrespectfully."

"I agree. I'm sorry, I have a hard time controlling my temper."

"Apology accepted. See to it that you have your temper under control. Reverend Benson, at the People of God, we try to keep our members calm and comfortable in every aspect. Inviting forty prostitutes and twenty drug dealers was a very dangerous and very intimidating act. Do you realize how hazardous that was to our members and to our church?"

John kept himself controlled and civil, "Yes sir, I do."

"Did you realize that at the time?"

"Yes sir."

"Then may I ask why you did a such foolish and unwise thing?"

"Because they were starving for Jesus."

Chuck looked around at the deacons and then replied, "We are not saying not to preach the gospel to those kind of people. We're simply saying to minister to those people outside of church."

John asked a question that he had been wondering for a while now, "Then what's the purpose of church?"

An unnatural silence fell upon the room. Everyone eyed each other. The question was so easy, yet no one could think of the answer. Chuck struggled for words, "A place where people can come and worship God."

"Right. So what's wrong with that?"

"Well, nothing is wrong with—"

"Exactly. So why won't you let me do that?"

Now Chuck and all the deacons were becoming very frustrated with their pastor. Chuck raised his voice, "The point is that we want you to do that, but do it in a fashion that will help the church, not destroy it."

John spoke slowly so that everyone heard what he said, "I'm just doing what's right."

A deacon spoke up, "Reverend Benson, you must remember that you're not running a youth gathering anymore. You're running a grown-up church now." Everyone nodded.

The words stung John like a thousand bee stings. His heart seemed to sink to his stomach. Was he right? John sunk down into his chair with every eye on him. He felt pathetic with the deacons and Chuck looking down at him as if he was a kid being punished.

* * *

John opened his bedroom door. Mary was already in bed and said wearily, "Hey."

"Hey." Then he walked to the sink, brushed his teeth, went to the bathroom, took his pills, and crawled into bed. He lay on his back and sighed, "I failed."

That caught Mary's attention. She turned to him, "Why on earth did you say that?"

"The church hates me."

"Hates you?"

"Yeah. I realize that all I'm doing is destroying it. They presented the facts to me. We're losing money fast, the congregation is decreasing in size, and pretty soon they're going to fire me." He looked at his wife, "I'm just doing what is right."

She nodded, "I know, I know you are. I've heard every one of your sermons since you started. And every one reminded me more and more of your teenage passion for God. It's not you that's failing; it's the church itself that's failing. You're steering it in the right direction, and the church wants to be steered in the wrong direction."

"I know they do. It's so hard these days just to do the right thing. You know?"

Mary nodded, "I know."

* * *

The next morning, John woke up before sunrise and decided to go ahead and do his morning routine. He walked into the kitchen with his bathrobe on and clicked on the lights. He turned on the coffee machine and made his way toward the front door. He unbolted it and took a deep breath in the morning air. Rubbing his eyes, he gazed all around him. Maybe he was steering the church in the wrong direction. Was that deacon right? Was being a pastor of a church different from leading a teenage gathering? But how could it be different? You're worshiping the same God. Then what's the point of church? To see how much money you can make? To design and build impressive buildings? To see how many people come? Does the heart of worship matter in big churches like that? Do I need to start doing what's best for the church even though the heart of worship would be gone?

John rubbed his eyes trying to comprehend his duty. No! He cannot do what's right for the church! He had to do what's right for God! John squinted his eyes at a car in his driveway. He did not have his glasses on so he had to step closer. There was an old, rusty Mercury Cougar parked on the driveway. Whose car was that? Well Mary had a…what did she have? He stopped amazed that he could not remember what kind of car his wife had. He thought. What was wrong with him? Well, okay, Amber drove a…wait, did Amber even have a car? She was sixteen so she was able to drive. But John couldn't remember if she had a car or not. He hit his forehead with his palm. Why could he not remember? Wait. Mary told him that Amber was on a date with some guy. Was that his car? If it was, then what was it doing here at 5:30

in the morning? That meant he was still here. For some reason, John was having a hard time thinking clearly. Then a thought popped in his mind. Oh no. He rushed back inside and walked through the dark hallway. There was Will's door cracked open with Will sleeping inside. Next to his door was Amber's. It was closed. John opened it. The bed was perfectly and tightly made. She was not in there. Across the hall was the guest room door. He put his sweaty hand on the doorknob, twisted it, and opened the door to the dark room. There was enough light to see—barely. There was Amber asleep in the guest room bed. John gasped. Sleeping right beside her was Jason. Both of them woke up shocked.

Amber gasped, "Dad…I…we—"

John's teeth clenched together. His heart was thumping and he could feel it about to explode out of his chest. He did not know what to think or to say. His blood pressure rose. "Who are you?" he growled at the top of his lungs.

Jason leaped out of bed fully clothed. At least he was dressed, "This is not what you think it is." He boldly walked right up to John.

"What do you think you were doing?"

"We weren't doing anything, I swear!"

John's words shot out of his mouth, "Don't lie to me! You were sleeping with my daughter!" Spit flew out of his mouth, his eyes bulged with anger and his lip quivered.

Jason held his ground, "You don't understand, she needs me."

He did not like that answer one bit, "Get out! Get out of my house!"

Jason just stood there with his feet planted in the thick carpet. Amber's voice squealed behind him, "Dad, don't do this! I love him!"

But John didn't listen to her. He looked directly into Jason's eyes and bellowed louder than ever, "Now!"

Jason saw the anger in the man's eyes and knew he was not joking. With one gulp, Jason walked out of the house. John looked back at Amber who stood on the floor in her pajamas. Her lip was quivering, her face was red, and tears streamed down her face. "How could you do that?" she shrieked, "He was the only one I loved! He gave me more love than you ever did! We weren't doing anything! I hate you! You and your stupid dying church!" She sprinted out of the room and into her room slamming the door behind her. John's angry expression diminished. His eyes turned glassy, his mouth dropped open in shame. He was hurt. Deeply, painfully hurt.

* * *

John sat on the edge of his bed staring at the wall. The evening sun projected a strong orange light against his face, as it went down. The bedroom door opened. Mary stepped in and closed it gently.

John looked up, "Still won't answer?"

Mary shook her head.

He exhaled, "Do you think I was too hard on her?"

"No! Not at all."

"I mean, her date spent the night with her. What was I supposed to do?"

"You handled that boy like you should of," she spoke softly, "I think what Amber needs right now is love."

"You're right." He had already given it a lot of thought. "I've been so busy lately and I totally understand how hard it was for her to move." His voice rose as he continued, "I have not given her any love or any attention ever since we moved here! I must take blame for the distance between us. She has every reason to hate me."

Mary sat down next to him. "It's my fault too," she admitted. "I mean I never asked her how her day was or who she was dating. I've been so zeroed out of her life."

John's depression was suddenly replaced with hope; "I'm going to talk to her right now. Let me just take my pills real quick."

A faint smile appeared on Mary's face, "That's a good idea."

He stood up and walked to the bathroom. He reached down on the wooden table to grab his pill bottles, but he just grabbed air. He looked down. All three were gone. John began searching all around the table, on the floor, and in the cabinets. He called behind him, "Honey, have you moved my pills?"

She hollered back, “No, I haven’t seen them.”

“Well, they’re not here.” John froze. His eyes widened. In one instant, he sprinted out of his room turning sharply into the hallway. He rushed down to Amber’s room and tried to twist the knob, but it was locked. He raced back to his room and flung open the closet.

Mary was puzzled, “What’s wrong?”

He grabbed a hanger and ran out of the room shouting, “She’s got my pills!”

Mary put her hand to her mouth and raced down the hall with him. They both stopped at Amber’s door. She kept her hand on her mouth as she watched John hurriedly untwist the metal hanger breathing rapidly. Soon the hanger turned into a straight metal rod. John stuck the end into the hole in the middle of the doorknob. With a few metallic clanks, the door swung open. John and Mary rushed inside to her bathroom. He stopped right at the door. Mary stopped right behind him and gasped.

Amber was sprawled on the floor with her sink running, and three empty pill bottles lying on the floor near her hand. There was no time to think or grieve. John quickly picked her up and swung her over his shoulder rushing outside.

Mary’s heart was racing. She could not think. She did not know what to do. She was almost paralyzed, but she managed to follow after John, "What are we going to do?"

"We're going to take her to the hospital! All we can do is get her there safely and pray!" he answered.

Will popped out of his bedroom and shouted in a panicked tone, "What happened?"

John quickly answered as he carried Amber to the front door, "Amber is really sick and we're taking her to the hospital. You stay here. We'll give you a call when we get there."

With that, he opened the back door to his car and placed her inside quickly. Then he ran to the driver door and got in. Mary got in on the passenger side. John put the car into gear and sped toward the closest hospital. Mary's eyes filled with tears. John looked at her, "Don't worry, they'll be able to help her." Then he turned his attention on the road and sped faster.

Suddenly, a sharp pain came to his head. He nearly screamed at the horrific pain. Putting his hand to his head, he could actually feel the tumor now. He could actually feel the deadly cancer dwelling inside his brain. Without the painkillers, he could now experience the black brain cancer itself creeping through his head, puncturing his skull, breeding like a multiplying band of warriors. John felt like his skull was about to explode, as he screamed in terror again.

Mary spoke in a trembling desperate voice, "Honey, do you want me to drive?"

The pain suddenly vanished, but he still felt the swelling of the plagued army. He replied, “No, I’m fine.” He looked back at Amber, still passed out in the back seat with her face drained and her heart working hard to pump blood.

They were almost there. Just a few more miles. Whiteness started developing on the periphery of John’s vision. He pressed the gas pedal harder. The whiteness started dominating his vision slowly. Blackness. “I can’t see, I’ve gone blind!” he exclaimed.

Mary grabbed the steering wheel, “I’ll pull over!” She yanked the steering wheel to the right and they veered into the grass. John let his foot off the gas pedal and slammed on the brakes. The car came to a stop, and they both jumped out. Still completely blind, John felt his way around the hood with tree branches slapping his face. He came around to the passenger door, felt for the handle, yanked it open, and got in. Mary slammed on the gas pedal and sped toward the hospital.

John knew that he was still blind, but his mind was on his daughter. He put his hands to his sightless eyes and ran his fingers through his hair. He could hear Mary sobbing right next to him. He wailed, “God, what have I done? My own daughter is trying to commit suicide because of me!”

Mary made a sharp turn. The traffic became denser and denser. John felt the car moving slower and slower until it stopped. They were behind a whole line of cars waiting for a red traffic light. Mary could not hold in her emotions any longer. She slammed her head down on the steering wheel and started crying bitterly. The sun was gone now and it was almost pitch dark. John tilted his head upward at heaven as he always did when he really needed God. He prayed aloud, "Lord, please help us."

Through the blackness, a streak of light pierced through. It started growing more until John could see the hospital right ahead! His eyesight started returning. He leaped out of the car in happiness exclaiming, "Thank you Lord!" He could not see clearly, but he could see well enough. John swung open the back door, lifted Amber over his shoulder, and ran to the hospital on foot.

He yelled at Mary, "Meet me there!" Maybe he was short, but he was still strong. His legs were strengthened with will power as he carried Amber.

John raced through the hospital parking lot. His legs started to burn, but he never slowed down. The cold wet air filled his lungs and stung his throat as each breath of visible air was exhaled from his mouth. The whiteness was still around his eyes and sound was like a freight train in his ears. His senses seemed to be shutting down and his whole body felt wobbly. The cancer was not going to win, he kept telling himself.

Finally, the double glass doors came into view. John gave it everything he had to push himself toward the doors. He approached them breathless. Too exhausted and lightheaded to open the door, he fell against it and pushed it open with his sheer body weight. He entered the lobby moving toward the front desk unsteadily, his face white. The front desk seemed to get farther and farther away. Although Amber was still over his shoulder, he felt like he was suddenly lighter. All the hospital noise seemed swallowed. The whiteness started dominating his eyesight again. In one desperate voice he yelled, "She's…overdosed!"

John's head was spinning and he felt even more light-headed. Speaking those words felt like a knife stabbing into his head at every syllable. He choked and vomited all over the floor. Everything turned white as his face met the hard floor.

Chapter 8

"Hey Will." Mary was calling on the hospital's wall telephone.

"Hey Mom."

"Are you okay?"

He answered, "Yeah, I'm fine."

"Well let me tell you the news. Uh, Amber swallowed all of Dad's pills today. She overdosed."

"But why did she take all those pills?" he asked.

Mary paused. Then taking a breath she answered, "Because Amber was having some problems in life so she tried to—" she could not believe she was explaining this so she just left it there, "She was just depressed. Anyway, she's unconscious still. The doctors are working on her to make her wake up. When she swallowed Dad's pills, he couldn't take them. And with his cancer, he can't function without them, so the doctors are working on him too." She could feel deep emotion rising in her. She could not let Will hear her like this so she finished, "I don't know what time I'll be home tonight, but it could be very late. Lock the doors. I love you, bye."

"Bye."

Mary hung up the telephone. She leaned against the wall overwhelmed and ran her fingers through her hair. Why is this happening?

"Mrs. Benson?"

Mary turned her head, still leaning on the wall, and looked at the plump nurse.

The nurse spoke in a soft merciful voice, "The surgeons have indicated that your daughter had swallowed almost three whole bottles of analgesics, anticonvulsants, and orticosteroids. Our surgeons are working on pumping the medication out of her stomach."

"Will she be okay?"

The nurse nodded uncomfortably, "Probably so. Overdoses are becoming increasingly common these days. However, the medications usually taken are over-the-counter pain relievers such as Advil, Motrin, Tylenol, and such. In this case, your daughter took potent prescription painkillers and brain seizure drugs."

Mary nodded.

The nurse flipped her notepad and looked up, "And the news about your husband. Brain cancer is very serious. Missing his medication can be very dangerous, causing accelerated digression. Has he been complaining of increased pain?"

Mary thought and shook her head, "No, not that much."

"Okay. Have you noticed any of his senses failing?"

"He was completely blind for a few minutes."

"Sudden headaches?"

She nodded, "Definitely, and he didn't hide that."

The nurse smiled to ease the tension, "Loss of memory?"

"Not that I know of."

"Have any trouble keeping his balance?"

Mary closed her eyes and thought, "He was stumbling a little bit when he carried my daughter."

She nodded, "Any seizures?"

She was a bit shocked when she heard that question, "No, not at all."

"And one last question, has he been vomiting?"

"No."

"Okay, thanks. Now do you mind if I ask you some personal questions regarding your daughter?"

"No, I don't mind."

"Okay. Do you have any idea why your daughter performed a suicidal act?"

Mary gulped, "Yes. Early this morning, my husband found her and her boyfriend asleep in our guest room bed together. My husband yelled at the boyfriend and made him leave like he should have. Amber got mad, told my husband that she hated him, and ran into her room and never came out for the rest of the day.

"My husband is a sensitive man so when she told him that she hated him, that just haunted him for the rest of the day. At about 6:oo today, he decided to have a nice calm conversation with her. But when he went to go take his pills, they were gone so he raced down to Amber's bathroom and found her passed out with his pill bottles on the bed next to her completely empty."

The nurse nodded understanding, "I see. Has she ever been depressed like this before?"

Mary shook her head, "No. She's always been a happy sweet girl. We just moved here from Tennessee last summer because my husband was asked to be the pastor of a church here. And ever since we moved, she's been, you know, depressed about the whole thing."

"I understand. I remember that age. Thanks for your cooperation Mrs. Benson. I'm sure we'll get all this worked out. I know it's been really tough for you."

Mary smiled, "Thanks."

John approached Mary, looking fine and acting fine. Mary saw him walking towards her and stood up trying to remain calm but unable to disguise the desperation in her voice, "Are you alright?"

He replied, "Yeah, I'm fine. How's Amber?"

Mary swallowed and answered, "The doctors think that she has about an eighty percent chance of being fine. But her case is more serious than others they deal with because she swallowed some serious stuff."

John nodded, "Let's just pray she'll be alright."

The same plump nurse approached them, "Sorry to interrupt, but your daughter has improved. She appears to be out of danger."

Mary and John sighed in relief. Then they both rushed to where Amber was. John opened the door. There was Amber lying there on the hospital bed. Machinery, wires, and tubes were everywhere. Her face was pale and her eyes seemed fearful.

Mary rushed over to her and knelt down by her bed speaking softly, "Honey, are you okay?"

She nodded.

John took Mary's place and knelt down speaking softy as well, "Look, I'm so sorry for not giving you the attention you've been needing." He waited for that to sink in and continued, "I know it's been really tough with everything that's going on. But I want you to know that I love you, and I always will. I promise I will show you more love from now on. Okay?"

Amber felt so guilty and so stupid; she didn't know what to say so she just nodded.

Mary leaned in over John, "You put your life and Dad's life into jeopardy. His cancer was attacking him and he fainted when he was—"

John interrupted, "Shh. It doesn't matter."

Amber fell back on her bed. She was now feeling painfully accountable.

John, Mary, and Amber walked into the black parking lot. Amber looked down as she walked.

After thinking deeply about the whole situation, she looked up at John and shouted, "Dad!"

He spun around, "Yes?"

Shameful, guilty tears filled her eyes as she ran towards him. She threw her arms around him embracing him with all her might and in barely audible voice whispered, "I love you, Dad."

Slowly, she felt his arms wrap around her—his arms of love. She knew a loving father was holding her.

* * *

It was weird going back to school for Amber for some reason. She was still thinking about what her father did for her. She just could not believe it. She could not believe that she had put him through so much extra pain.

She strolled on the sidewalk watching other students walking around carrying their full backpacks to their cars. Something caught her eye. Walking towards her were Jason and Meagan. They looked the same except Jason had his arm around Meagan and she had her arm around him. They were talking, smiling, and laughing while Amber just stared. They approached Amber and almost ran over her. Both kept on grinning as Jason turned to her, "Sorry, Amber. I can't be with a preacher's daughter." There was no seriousness in his voice as if he did not care about her or any relationship that they had had. Meagan was smiling and laughing too. Meagan. Amber thought she was her friend.

Jason and Meagan walked passed her leaving her dejected. A chill ran up her spine and she suddenly felt cold and naked. Her heart sank to her stomach and seemed to stop beating. A lump clogged her throat and her breath exhaled in quivering pants. She felt alone with no one to turn to. She especially felt used. Then her father's love returned to her mind. God's love. Her lips formed a smile as the thought came to her. God's love.

* * *

About a week later, John walked up to the podium at the People of God. Chuck still sat back in his special chair observing every move he made. The congregation was even smaller than last Sunday. But there were more street people than ever. Chuck did not like that at all.

John opened up in a strident voice, "Where did all our members go? Are they not serious enough to come and worship? Many of you may not realize this, but this church has grown." He was looking at the prostitutes and drug dealers. "Look at the improvement. Look at all these people in the pews who are thirsty for God. Many of you want some music at the services. I totally agree. We need some music because it helps us worship. Anyway, whoever has musical talent and wants to use it for God, see me after the service. Mr. Freeman wants me to announce to all of you our financial progress. When Reverend Johnson left, this church had thirty million dollars. Now we have dropped all the way down to five thousand. But why does money matter? Why?"

A man in the congregation blurted out, "Because it helps this church grow, and that's what we need!"

John raised his voice, "How does money make this church grow? It doesn't! What makes the church grow is the power of God. Not money. If we let God have this church, it will grow in ways that matter to Him!"

Chuck rubbed his eyes in misery.

John continued, "Each one of us in this sanctuary is created in God's image. We are all special to Him. Do you believe that? You better because that means God has a mission in all of our lives. We are unworthy, but we are not worthless. If God created us, then we must have worth. Our lives have worth, but we don't know it. Why? Because we allow ourselves to clutter our lives with so much corruption and worrying and sin that we don't see our mission. We don't see our worth. How long are we going to allow ourselves to be cluttered like this?

"Every church has a mission." The cancer. "We as a church family need to accomplish that mission." The sharp pain returned to John's head. He stopped, squinted his face, and held his hand to his head for a few seconds. He started screaming in pain. It went away as John straightened up. The crowd stared at him while Chuck looked at him strangely.

John continued, "The heart—" He paused. The whiteness started returning to his eyes. The same dizzy feeling returned. All his senses started deadening. "The heart—" His legs grew weak, his voice was being lost and swallowed by a freight train. "The heart of worship!" he cried. His head was spinning. The congregation started mumbling to each other. Chuck just kept watching. John fainted and his body collapsed on the ground.

Chuck rose from his chair and ran over to John. He rolled him over on his back and checked his pulse. Then he called out, "Call an ambulance!" The ushers started shuffling out the doors and the crowd started rising from the their chairs. Murmuring filled the room.

* * *

John's eyes opened and adjusted to the bright light above his head. He was lying on his back. At first, he did not know where he was until he shifted his eyes around the room. He was lying down on a white bed with a white sheet over him. The room was rather small with a single window on the opposite side that displayed the rain and the gray sky. Medical machines were everywhere. He felt something on his wrists. He looked down and saw intravenous lines in his wrists and a cord that ran from his chest to a machine that displayed a black monitor with a squiggly green line etching across it. *Beep...beep.* John's head was still spinning and he still could not think straight.

The door opened and a middle-aged man dressed in white entered. He looked at John. "Oh, you're awake now," he said casually.

John found words and spoke, "What happened?"

The doctor walked towards him, "You fainted because your brain stopped functioning."

Now John knew what was going on. He went to the point, "How much longer will I live?"

The doctor paused and cleared his throat, "Well, John, if you want to hear it bluntly, you're not going to live much longer. Any day now."

John nodded. He was ready for that kind of answer. "Okay," he said evenly.

"Would you like to see your family?"

John looked at him.

"They're right outside," he said pointing his thumb towards the door.

John nodded, "Sure."

"Okay, I'll be right back." With that, the doctor opened the door and left the room. The sound of the rain and the constant beeping returned. A low roll of thunder vibrated the window. John stared at the ceiling mumbling under his breath, "God, take care of my family."

The door opened and three bodies appeared. John had to adjust his languid eyes to focus on them. There was Mary looking stressed, Amber looking stunned, and Will with a petrified look on his face.

Mary hurried over to John's bed and knelt down, "John, are you alright?"

John tried his best to act normally, "Yeah, I'm fine."

Will walked over to the bed while Amber followed. He looked down at John on the bed. "Dad, you can't leave us," he said sorrowfully.

John pressed his lips together and formed a half smile, "Son, I'm going to have to soon."

Amber entered the conversation, "But how can God do this to you? I mean after all you've done?"

John looked at her, "I don't know. Sometimes God does things that we don't understand. That is part of His plan."

She was not convinced, "But still, why is He letting you die?"

He spoke softly and tenderly, "I have to die sometime. I can't live forever. I've lived my life."

Will interrupted, "But how am I going to get through school?"

"Will, you don't need me to get through school. You need God. He'll help you. Be a disciple. Make a difference in your school."

Will nodded, "Okay."

* * *

Another strike of lightning lit the sky. Inside the People of God's conference room, the board of deacons and Chuck sat at the long table. One of the deacons stood, "Mr. Freeman, because our current pastor, Reverend Benson, is in critical condition and is expected to pass away any day now, the board has held a secret vote on the call of a new pastor. We need someone with experience, who can rebuild this church, and who can give it back its former reputation. The only man capable of this position will have to be you, Mr. Freeman. We, as the board of deacons, have decided to pronounce you pastor of the People of God and give you the title, Reverend Freeman." The deacons smiled and clapped as the man sat. Chuck stood with his chin up proudly.

* * *

"Mom, how did you and dad meet?" Amber and Mary were sitting in the two chairs by John who was sleeping. Will was sitting by them and moved in closer to hear the answer.

Mary turned her head towards her and answered, "Well, in ninth grade, we were both freshman. We didn't know each other that well. I mean, I knew who he was and he knew who I was. He was, you know, kind of quiet and kind of unnoticeable. But all the girls thought he was cute including me. In tenth grade, he set up a small Bible study with only like eight people. At first, no one knew about it, but soon it became bigger and bigger until everyone knew about it. I thought it was the coolest thing anyone could have done in school, and I really respected Dad for doing that. So, I started talking to him, and he was a really nice sweet guy. We got to know each other real well, and we went on a few dates with each other.

"Well his Bible Study grew to be a gigantic gathering place and caused a real revival in our school. You already know all about that though."

Amber nodded.

"Anyway, we both graduated from high school. He went to a college in North Carolina and I stayed in Tennessee and went to college there. But we still kept in touch, and he would drive to my college all the time. We were still dating until one day we were taking a romantic walk through a park somewhere. We were talking about movies or something and just out of nowhere John just said, 'Hey, do you want to me marry me?' Just like that. It was so casual, and he asked it like he would any other question. But I knew he was very serious because he had that serious look on his face. You know, that look when he would look straight into your eyes. I was so excited and I said yes."

Amber smiled, "Cool."

Mary's happy expression turned serious, "But what I respect in him most of all is his strong will. He has always been like that and he still is. No matter what anyone says, he never compromises his beliefs. No matter how hard the trail is, as long as it is right, he never turns back. It did get him into a lot of trouble though. I remember one day in biology class, Dad had a big yelling fight with the teacher about evolution right in the middle of class. I mean, Dad was standing right in front of his face just yelling about how stupid evolution is. That got him suspended from school for a while. It went on his record. It's like he never stops walking along steep cliffs. Maybe Dad does go a little overboard with what he believes in, but he never gives up. He never stops." Mary wiped her eyes. "Something that he always said in high school and he still says today is, 'I'm just trying to do what's right.' You've heard him say that before I'm sure." Mary sniffed.

Amber put her arm lovingly around her mother, "I'm going to miss him." She glanced over at Will who was sitting there on a little table minding his own business thinking about John. The heart monitor still beeped. Curiously, Amber stood up and walked towards John's bed to get a good look at it. She lost her breath. The green line was almost perfectly straight with one single hump. She hollered back, "Mom, he's barely breathing!"

Mary immediately stood up and rushed over with Will following. All three looked down at John. He was barely alive. Inside, he was struggling for his life. With a desperate voice he spoke, "Whatever you do," he coughed, "Don't ever lose your faith. Don't ever! I love you all."

Tears streamed down Mary's face as she knelt down. She took his hand. It was ice cold and clammy. She spoke in a quivering voice, "Please don't leave us."

John's head felt like it had a knife in it. The cancer was dominating his brain. The war was ending. The cancerous army was standing victorious with its black gummy bodies and deadly swords in their hands. They planted a cancerous flag into the mushy brain and shouted in triumph over the cells that were defeated.

John looked deep into Mary's eyes with his serious look. He could not think clearly enough to say anything much so his lips formed an "I love you." Then he slowly placed his head on his pillow staring upward. His cold hand fell from Mary's hand. The heart monitor displayed a perfectly straight line. John's face was motionless. His opened eyes still had the soft puppy look to them. His graying wavy hair reminded Mary of his black wavy hair in high school. His face was pale, and although he had a few wrinkles in his skin, his face still contained the youthful look he had always had.

Was he a good pastor? Some would say yes, some would say no. However, Mary knew that she was looking down at the greatest pastor she had ever known. The whole family broke into tears. Mary wrapped her arms around Amber while Will cried on the bed. John lay there lifeless with his eyes staring up at heaven.

* * *

The new Reverend Chuck Freeman walked up proudly to the podium with his chest held high. The congregation was the same size as it was last Sunday, but Chuck knew he was going to restore the crowd and bring back the members. He was going to restore this church and give it back the reputation it formerly knew with Reverend Johnson. He was going to make profits higher than ever. He was going to make this church the biggest church in the world.

Chuck scanned the crowd in the pews. Most of them were city scum and only a few were usual members. He knew he was going to change all that. In a happy voice he spoke, "Good morning. As many of you know, Reverend Benson passed away from brain cancer a few days ago. It was very sad seeing our brother in Christ leave this world, but he is in heaven right now so praise the Lord that he is home. Uh, since Reverend Benson passed away, I will be taking his place as pastor of this church. I'm very excited, we're going to work on building this church to the maximum with God's help. Uh, one announcement I would like to make. The gift shop is now reopened for all of you to enjoy so when you leave today, let's shop, shop, shop!" There was an uncanny happiness in his voice when he said that.

Chuck continued, "Now, as the new pastor of this church, I would like to raise money in this church and attract more people to this church, because the more people who come, the better the church. We want this church to be the best it can be," he raised his voice in excitement, "And how are we going to do that?"

"The heart of worship," said a voice in the pews.

Chuck's smile dropped. He looked out into the crowd and saw one of the black drug dealers standing on his feet facing Chuck. It was Ernie. Chuck did not feel so powerful anymore. He cleared his throat, "Uh, what I was—"

A prostitute stood up with Ernie.

Chuck fell silent as he watched Ernie and the prostitute standing up.

A woman who was a usual church member stood up. Another woman who was a member stood up. Two men who were members stood up together. More prostitutes, more drug dealers, and more members stood. Soon most of the congregation stood. Their chests were high, their chins were up, and their faces were set. Ernie shouted out, "The heart of worship is all that matters!"

Sweat rolled down Chuck's forehead. His mouth dropped open in shock. Most of the people stood with their faces serious and their bodies straight. He tried ordering, "Please take a seat."

It did no good. The congregation still stood with Ernie. They were standing in honor of John Benson. More importantly, they were standing in honor of God.

The Heart of Worship

When the music fades
All is stripped away, and I simply come
Longing just to bring
Something that's of worth
That will bless Your heart
I'll bring You more than a song
For a song in itself
Is not what You have required
You search much deeper within
Through the way things appear
You're looking into my heart

I'm coming back to the heart of worship
And it's all about You
It's all about You, Jesus
I'm sorry, Lord, for the thing I've made it
And it's all about You
It's all about You, Jesus

King of endless worth
No one could express

How much You deserve
Though I'm weak and poor
All I have is Yours, every single breath
I'll bring You more than a song
For a song in itself
Is not what You have required
You search much deeper within
Through the way things appear
You're looking into my heart

I'm coming back to the heart of worship
And it's all about You
It's all about you, Jesus
I'm sorry, Lord, for the thing I've made it
And it's all about You
It's all about You, Jesus

9 780595 157167